# A NICE, RELAXING
# SEA CRUISE

*Bob~*
*Great meeting*
*you & the WWA*
*Conference*
*Enjoy*

DALE R. BOTTEN

ILLUSTRATIONS BY
JEFF FRISKE

PAGE PUBLISHING, INC.
New York, NY

First originally published by Page Publishing, Inc. 2017

ISBN 978-1-64138-057-7 (Paperback)
ISBN 978-1-64138-058-4 (Digital)

Printed in the United States of America

# CHAPTER ONE

I turned my 1977, sort-of-new little red Volkswagen left onto Welford Avenue, as per the gas station attendant's somewhat confusing instructions. I had wondered, as the mousy old man in the blue suit mumbled and grunted his advice, if the government shouldn't establish regulations concerning the giving of directions by gas station attendants. It could be called The Federal Bureau of Directions Information and could be presided over by a chimpanzee.

So raucous was my laughter upon this reflection that I nearly collided with the Frankenstein monster himself. It was only by God's good graces I happened to be going slow enough to brake in time. In the stark glare of my headlights, I could see that the four-foot monster was being followed across the street by the Blob and a Hobo, with a petite fairy princess bringing up the rear. Rolling down the car window, I called to them.

"Excuse me, there! Mister Frankenstein!"

The children stopped and turned back to me.

"Could you give me some directions, please?" I continued. "I'm looking for 1524 Buford Drive! It's the old Hudson house!"

Frankenstein dropped his jaw—just about to his knees; the Hobo dropped his pack; and it was difficult to tell just what the Blob (being a blob) dropped, but the fairy princess hid nervously behind him and stared at me incredulously.

"The H-H-H-Hudson house?" stammered Frankenstein. "Sure, but it won't do you any good. There's nobody there. Been empty for years."

"Yes, I know." I laughed. "I'm James Hudson. I own it now."

"You own the Hudson house?" exclaimed the little princess. "But...it's...it's haunted!"

I laughed again. "Yes. That's what I hear. Now, if you'll just tell me where it is, I'll go and greet my new family of ghosts."

"Sure," replied Frankenstein. "Just go on straight two blocks. That's Buford Drive. Then, turn right, and it's about two miles down, on the left. But I sure wouldn't want to go there at night, if I was you...especially not tonight."

"Well," I said, reaching into my pocket for some dollar bills. "Thank you for your concern, but it's imperative I get there as soon as possible." Stretching my arm out the window to its God-given limit, I offered a bill for each of the children. "Here. Each of you have an ice cream on me...and happy Halloween."

With all the caution of today's paranoid society, Frankenstein advanced only as close as necessary to retrieve the Georges from my hand and then retreated back to the sidewalk.

"Gee, thanks, Mister Hudson," he said, followed closely by the others, "and good luck."

"Ya," chimed the Blob, "you're gonna need it."

*The house on Buford Drive...where it all began*

Straight two blocks, turn right and down two miles on the left. Now, why couldn't the gas station attendant do that well? As I started up again, I looked about me. It was a perfect All Hallows' Eve. A big, bold harvest moon hung suspended in a cosmic vacuum, like a plump, ripe pumpkin that was ready for the press...and nearly the same color. Harmless, high cirrus clouds drifted about the atmosphere, obliterating most of the stars and occasionally blanking out Luna herself. There was a light breeze about; just enough to give a whispered voice, eerie and foreboding, to the trees and a chill to the night air.

I thought of my own childhood, too many years before, and the carefree fun of Halloweens long past. Perhaps that's the reason I was there on that road to an old, beat-up house I'd never seen. Perhaps that nearly forgotten boyhood feeling of excitement and adventure was what I'd hoped to recapture by such an improbable undertaking. Did I really believe Great-Great-Great-Grandfather Hudson was a pirate? And if that be true, did he alone know the whereabouts of a fabulous treasure? A fool's false hope. And yet, fool that I am, there was something buried deep within my breast, beneath my very soul, that gave credence to this most prodigious possibility. It was, undoubtedly, the same inner faith that fathered belief in Santa Claus and love for the Easter bunny and perhaps stepchild to that supreme faith in Almighty God himself.

Whatever its source, its effect was to start my heart beating like a trip hammer as I pulled up in front of the old house. It was curiously isolated on Buford Drive, the nearest dwelling being nearly a block away. It must have been from one of these, while still several blocks away, that I had seen the light shining. Or else, it was a streetlamp reflection, for as I gazed now up at the venerable structure, there was no hint of illumination from any of the loosely boarded windows.

I rummaged through my glove compartment for my genuine Boy Scouts of America flashlight and the notes I had taken from Great-Great-Great Grandfather's secret will, which the trust company had kept secret until such occasion occurred, as ancestor Hudson directed it should, when the will could be revealed. Thus armed, I proceeded through the creaky front gate and up the uneven walk to the front door.

It was, I noted, not an overly impressive building in size, as I had expected it would be. I guessed its two and a half stories to accommodate perhaps five bedrooms and two baths with a large attic that would, hopefully, contain the book of information I had driven nearly two thousand miles to find. In his first will, James Bartholomew Hudson (the First) had directed that the house be closed, following the death of his beloved wife, but that the trust company handling his estate should see to the upkeep of the building and grounds, pending enactment of his second will. But only the trust company knew when that should be, and they were sworn to secrecy. Of course, being a man of considerable means, James the First saw to the financial comfort of all his children...the soft-hearted old pirate. This house on Buford Avenue was the only thing left unassigned, and nobody (save the trust company) knew why.

Fumbling in my pocket for the keys that Mr. Jasper (the handler of the estate) had included with the will, I inserted one of them into the lock and turned it. But when I turned the knob, I found the door still to be locked. I turned the key again in the opposite direction and heard the lock disengage. Hmmmmm. That meant the door was already unlocked.

As if to foretell some impending danger, a dark, ominous cloud suddenly crossed the bright Halloween moon, and the wind began to race the earth in earnest. I opened the door, which, as the front door of any self-respecting haunted house should, creaked and groaned most pitifully—as if I were disturbing the pain-wracked bones of some ancient living being. My flashlight beam searched the wall for the electric light switch (a modern innovation added by Great-Great-Great Grandmother Hudson sometime after her husband's death in 1902). As I flicked the obsolete switch and the hallway entrance became bathed in the glow of days gone by, I was glad I had the foresight to wire ahead and have the light company restore power to the building. That, I reasoned, was also why I had found the front door unlocked. The meter man had simply forgotten to relock it. An uncommon occurrence, but entirely possible. This considerably eased the apprehension that had built up in my active imagination.

For being vacant nearly sixty years, the interior of the house looked in remarkably good shape. There was, of course, an accumulation of dust on those fixtures uncovered that would drive any diligent housekeeper straight into the clutches of demon rum. Bent on discovering the type of wood the spiral staircase that was located opposite the front door was made of, I took in a deep breath and blew as hard as I could. Then, I coughed and sneezed and cried and cursed and did all of those things one might expect from such a less-than-intelligent maneuver. Any ghost who had yet to learn of my presence was now assuredly informed of it. I did, however, learn that the staircase, beautifully preserved under some durable varnish, was made of sturdy oak wood; at least, to my untrained eye, that's what it appeared to be. A sailor's appreciation for seaworthy wood had apparently carried over to James's land-locked days very well.

Though not of a mansion's proportion, this house was definitely not cracker-box cheap.

After proper inspection of the hallway entrance, I proceeded on a self-guided tour of the major downstairs rooms. It was like stepping into an antique store. Finely crafted furniture of solid mahogany was adorned with ornaments of teakwood and brass (the more expensive gold and silver items had apparently been removed to a safer place...or stolen), and in each room was built a stone fireplace of a size proportional to its surroundings. It was, indeed, a magnificently crafted building. I considered myself wealthy in just possessing such a home, let alone one with a treasure map hidden somewhere within its antique frame.

With that thought a reminder of my original mission, I bounded up the circular stairway to the second floor. Finding a light switch similar to the one downstairs, I was soon making my way through the bedchambers and baths, merely acquainting myself with the relative proximity of the various rooms. This done, I stopped to consult my notes on the will, the document itself being too old and fragile to be carried about. The book I sought, the one wherein I might find the exact location of the treasure, was supposedly locked inside a metal box, inside an oaken chest. James the First certainly did have a passion for oak.

Now, if I were an oak chest, where would I hide? Of course, either in the basement or in the attic. Oak being as heavy as it is, the chest would probably be in the basement. But James the First being as crafty as he apparently was, the chest was undoubtedly in the attic. Besides, the attic was closer. The attic door was easy to locate, since it was one of the few along the narrow upstairs hallway I had not investigated. Vainly, I searched the stairwell for another light switch. Perhaps there was one farther up. Slowly, cautiously, I made my hesitant way up the steep steps, toward the black nothingness.

In all the world, there is nothing, with the possible exception of a graveyard at midnight on All Hallows' Eve, that will chill the spine and cause the human patellae to come together with such great rapidity and strength, more than the darkened attic of a haunted house. Suddenly, I remembered. This *was* Halloween! And glancing at my cheap electric Timex, I discovered that it *was* nearly the bewitching hour. I stopped. Perhaps it *would* be better to come back in the morning, when I was less tired from my long journey.

"Poppycock!" I muttered to myself. "Am I a man, or am I a mouse?"

## That ugly, beautiful gargoyle

Knowing the answer to that question, I proceeded up the stairs anyway. Slowly, step by frightening step, my genuine Boy Scouts of America flashlight and I braved the unknown darkness that lay between reality and imagination.

Now, let me say this: I'm sure whoever put that stone gargoyle at the head of the stairs didn't really intend that I should slam my head into the low door jam on my panic-stricken way out; or that, in my pain-ridden confusion, I should forget the front gate was only low enough to accommodate the passage of one leaping leg over it at a time; or that, once I had freed my impaled body from the gate's picket slats and reached the haven of my car, I should have discovered my keys locked inside. I'm sure he foresaw none of this. But as I collapsed onto the running board, trying to decide whether I should pass out first or puke first, that little bit of insight was of no comfort at all.

Presently, my head hurting too much to throw up and the rest of my body certainly aching too badly to pass out, I looked back at the house. Perhaps it was the headache or just the overactive imagination of the frightened little boy that had surfaced within me, but I could have sworn that house was laughing at me. It seemed as if I could hear the peals of laughter and guffaws of Great-Great-Great Grandfather Hudson ringing through the Halloween night. Or was it just my ears that were ringing? Today, I like to think the former; but at the time, I really didn't care which. If laughter were a toxicant, I was surely infected with a near-lethal dose. 'Til the tears dropped in pools about me, I ha-ha'd, ho-ho'd and generally made an adult ass of myself. But in that laughter, the pain subsided; and with it, the terror of a childhood mind.

Luckily, I carried with me an extra set of keys for the car and quickly recovered my forgotten ones. Soon, armed this time with a boy's flashlight and a man's constitution, I reentered Hudson house to resume my search, taking care this time to leave the gate open... just in case. Upon reaching the attic stairway, I opened the door—which, in my chaotic flight, I must have slammed shut behind me—and tramped boldly up the stairs. This time, I walked directly to that ugly stone creature in the attic and smiled.

"Good evening, sir," I said. "Mind if I look around?"

There seeming to be no objection from this one-gargoyle peanut gallery, I proceeded to do just that. The amount and variety of white-elephant (there may have been one of those too) antiques in that attic would set any dealer's chops to drooling. There was an enormous amount of ship's paraphernalia: lanterns, an old compass, and even a ship's wheel that stood as tall as a man. All this was in addition to the usual variety of nineteenth century household items one might expect. But these were mere trinkets to my greedy soul. The prize I sought was far greater than some rusty piece of the past.

Finally, after searching for quite some time, I found what must be the chest, nestled far back in a corner by a dressmaker's form (which looked and sounded remarkably like a girl I once knew). At any rate, my shaking hands groped in my pocket once again for the ring of keys from the trust company. There were five in all. One I knew fit the front door, and the other large key was meant for the back door. That left me with three chances for a proper fit. True to my gambling luck, it was my third choice that unlocked the chest. Inside were crammed those small bits of personal memorabilia that bespeak a man's life; his joys and sorrows, his loves and hates, his successes and failures. All entombed in one five-foot by two-foot by two-foot oaken chest. I wished I had time to examine them all, to find out more about my most remarkable great-great-great grand-father, James Bartholomew Hudson the First. Carefully, I laid each item aside, until I had uncovered a small metal box. Fingers numb with excitement fumbled to open the small lock. Opening the lid, I found a book bound in leather, with these words printed on the cover: "THE DIARY OF JAMES BARTHOLOMEW HUDSON" and the date "1839."

So overcome with expectation was I that my clumsy hands dropped the flashlight. As I reached to pick it up, I noticed something pooled on the floor nearby, but not touching the flashlight. Liquid, red liquid. It appeared to have run down from behind the trunk. Blood? No...God. Please, let it not be blood...please. Slipping the book into my coat pocket, I picked up the flashlight. Petrified with fear, I forced myself to trace the substance to its source. *WHAM!* The sound of the closing trunk lid echoed through my mind as I gazed behind the oaken box.

This time, there would be no slamming my head into the low door jam, no half-hearted attempts at leaping the front gate and no mirth at all; for a child's harmless fright had given way to a man's mortal terror. Behind the trunk was the freshly slain body of a man, eyes open wide in deathly anguish, whose throat had been slit from ear to ear.

# CHAPTER TWO

Police Lieutenant Trevor told me I was quite unintelligible when the officers found me. I had been doing seventy-five in a forty-five mile-per-hour zone. I had no idea my VW was capable of that kind of speed. According to the arresting officers, I collapsed after I got out of the car; and when they picked me up, I clung so tightly they had to handcuff me to keep me away from them.

By the time we reached the police interrogation room, I had calmed down somewhat and was able to blurt out my bizarre tale to the lieutenant. Almost by instinct, an instinct finely honed by many years of correcting other people's mistakes, Trevor's first move was to order a squad dispatched to the house. Then, accompanied by a lanky scarecrow of an officer, we drove in a black-and-white back to the Hudson house. I remember thinking in between Trevor's questions, what a nightmare this harmless children's festival had turned out to be. Halloweens were never like this when *I* was a child. I mean sure, we soaped old man Krockmeir's windows and knocked over Murphy's outhouse (How were we supposed to know it was occupied?). But...murder? Come on. The thought simply never occurred to us. Perhaps the children of today are just too advanced for their years. Trick or treat certainly doesn't mean what it used to.

"You say your name is Hudson, and you own the place now?" Trevor's words snapped me back to reality.

"Huh? Oh, yes. That's right. I inherited it from my great-great-great-grandfather." As I replied, I studied Lieutenant Trevor. His eyes were deep-set and the brows above them bushy and graying, as was what was left of his hair. He had a square-cut jaw, and a nose that seemed somehow to match.

Sergeant Scarecrow turned around. "How come he waited so long to give that thing away? Real estate company been watchin' it like a hawk longer 'n I can remember."

"According to the terms of the will," I answered, "the house could go only to the next direct descendent to bear the full name of James Bartholomew Hudson."

"And the contents of the will were kept secret so nobody would name his kid James Bartholomew Hudson just to get the house?"

"Right." I looked at the sergeant with a quizzical gaze. "But how did you know?"

"Heck." He grinned. "Folks around here been tryin' to figure out what's in that will for years. Just put the pieces together."

The lieutenant, who'd been thinking very deeply, spoke up. "What'd he look like?"

"Oh, I don't know," I replied. "I never saw him."

Trevor's eyes went wide. "You never saw him?"

"No."

"Then, how did you know he was dead?"

"Well, for starters, he was born in 1805. That would make him roughly one hundred seventy years old. Don't you think that's a little improbable? After all, he was only human."

"Who?"

"Great-Great-Great-Grandfather, of course."

Trevor looked disgusted with me. "I meant the dead body you found in the attic!"

"Oh," I said, my voice falling. I'd tried to forget that. "Well, I don't remember exactly. His eyes were awfully big, and he had a big hole in his throat." My fingers traced a line across my throat from one ear to the other. "From here to here."

"Very informative," Trevor said facetiously. "We'll see when we get up there."

That disquieting event was literally just around the corner. As the squad car approached the front of Hudson house, I felt a trembling in my knees, a pain in my head and a Gordian knot in my queasy little stomach. I hoped I wouldn't throw up all over the lieutenant.

There were two squads already there—lights flashing and all. One uniformed officer was talking on his radio, while another was questioning a small but curious crowd of neighbors dressed in an assortment of nighties and bathrobes that would do any Halloween trickster proud. One somewhat stout middle-aged lady still sported a mudpack (which may have improved her appearance considerably) and curlers the size of oil drums. As I drew near, flanked by two policemen, she stepped boldly out in front of me, her several chins flapping wildly.

"That's him! That's him, Officer!" She squealed, her fat little body jiggling with excitement. "That's the guy I saw prowling around here tonight! That's the guy I saw sneak into the house...and...and a little while later, he comes runnin' out just a yellin' and a hootin' and a laughin' like a madman." Her beady little eyes stared a hole right through me. "What'd he do? Kill somebody? What'd he do?"

Lord, I'm a peace-loving man, certainly not prone to arguments and insults; but this time, temptation and love of social justice utterly destroyed my willpower.

"Excuse me, madam," I said in my most formal, courteous voice, "haven't we met somewhere before? I think it was in a nightmare. Oh yes, that's it. It was at your castle in the haunted forest in the Land of Oz. Say, I thought Dorothy melted you?" I said it, and I'm glad. As we entered the house, I could still hear her demanding that I be arrested for something or other. I think it was for insulting a witch without a license.

Inside, we were met by another officer who was just descending the circular stairway.

"What'dya find?" Trevor queried.

The officer grinned. "Oh, we found a body, all right...of sorts." What a morbid sense of humor I thought that man to have, and rather ill-timed too.

"Let's have a look," Trevor replied, following the officer up the stairs. Reluctantly, I went next with Sergeant Scarecrow acting as a rear guard. At the entrance to the attic, I balked a little but forced myself to continue. Trevor beamed a flashlight about. There, for the third time, I encountered that same grotesque gargoyle—pointy ears, pointy face, and pointy head. I thought perhaps he belonged in Washington. Only this time, he seemed to be grinning at me...almost mocking me. I wondered what he knew that I didn't.

I was soon to find out. Both policemen beamed their lights behind the trunk. I stared, incredulous. It was a body all right...the body of a male mannequin, eyes wide open and staring right at me. The blood? There certainly was a lot of red stuff, but it wasn't blood. Lieutenant Trevor leaned over and picked up an empty can of red paint. I felt my face flush hot with embarrassment and perplexing wonder.

"But...but I *saw* him! It was a man...a real, live...uh, dead man! He had his throat slit wide open, and there was blood...real blood... all over!" The officers were grinning, and Sergeant Scarecrow was trying very hard not to laugh, his long and bony cheeks puffing out like an excited blowfish. Lieutenant Trevor was not amused. He looked down at the mannequin, then back at me.

"Mister Hudson," he said calmly, "in an attic so crowded with junk, do you think it possible you might have accidentally knocked the paint can over, and it popped the cover off?" I fumbled for my words.

"Well, uh...yes, I suppose so..."

"And the mannequin does have red paint all over its throat."

"Well, yes...yes, it does; but that's not what I saw..."

"And it *is* Halloween."

Realizing argument was going to be of no use at all, I capitulated and began apologizing profusely for causing such needless furor. Trevor cut me off.

"That's all right, Mister Hudson. As the bard has said, 'There are more things in heaven and earth than are dreamt of in your philosophy.'" He winked. "Especially on Halloween."

His knowledge of Shakespeare surprised me. He looked like Dick Tracy dressed like Columbo and spouted Shakespeare like Sherlock Holmes. Quite a curious mixture, this man named Trevor. I wondered how skillfully he handled his constabulary duties. Did he really think I couldn't tell the difference between a mannequin and a human body? Well, perhaps I couldn't.

When we stepped out onto the front porch, I noticed the crowd was mostly dispersed. That is, except for my fat little female friend, the Creature from the Black Lagoon. She was still trying to pin the Saint Valentine's Day Massacre on me. As I locked the front door, Trevor stopped and turned back to me.

"Mister Hudson," he offered, sounding now much like a thoughtful philosopher. "When I was a rookie cop, sitting on a motorcycle, I pulled this old guy over for speeding. As I recall, he was about eighty, and his wife looked older than that. When I asked him where the hell he was going so fast, he said he was taking his wife to the hospital. I thought they might need an escort, so I asked him what the problem was." Trevor paused for a moment, as if he were waiting for me to beg him to continue. I didn't, but he continued anyway. "Well, sir, that man looked me straight in the eye and told me his wife was pregnant."

My laughter drowned out the lieutenant's next sentence, but he kept going in all seriousness. "That was about the most ludicrous thing I'd ever heard," he continued. "I figured anybody with a story like that deserved one break, so I let him go with just a warning." I got the feeling Lieutenant Trevor was getting at something...something not exactly complimentary to my vehicular control proficiency. At least, I hadn't hit anything. Trevor took in a long breath. "But before I let him go, I told him that the next time I caught him speeding like that, his wife had better have one on her lap and one in the oven about to pop." I wanted to laugh out loud again but thought better of it.

"Mister Hudson," Trevor said, putting his hand on my shoulder in a very fatherly move, "the next time you do seventy-five in a for-ty-five mile-an-hour zone, you'd damn well better have either a dead body or a pregnant little old lady with you. Understood?"

I swallowed the stifled laugh that had caught in my throat. "Perfectly, Lieutenant."

The other officers and Sergeant Scarecrow were already out the gate, when Lieutenant Trevor and I descended the porch steps. Mrs.

Butterball was still at it. What a turkey. I heard her mumbling some-thing about my sitting down on the running board of my car and laughing maniacally. Down her throat was one of the more polite places I wanted to stuff that mudpack she was wearing. Just then, I stopped and looked back at the house. Perhaps it was Great-Great-Great-Grandfather putting ideas in my head, or perhaps the pres-sures of the evening had lowered my usually high tolerance level, but my eye caught directly upon an old broom standing by the front door. Most of its straws had long since either rotted off or been swept away with the winds of time, but it was still recognizable as a broom.

I turned and walked back up the steps. Seizing the broom, I carried it out the front gate. As I approached her, my tormentor addressed me again. "Are you really James Bartholomew Hudson? What're you doin' here this late at night? Bet you're lookin' for the treasure, ain't ya...well, ain't ya? You sure you didn't kill nobody?"

"Here!" I said curtly, thrusting the broom into what technically was a hand, but I swear looked more like the claw of a giant sand crab. "You seem to have forgotten this! Now, may I suggest you climb onto it and fly back to your own haunted house before you find out that it has become deeply imbedded as an integral appendage of your considerable personage! Good night, madam!"

With that, I turned sharply and stalked toward the squad car that was waiting to take me back to my own vehicle. The driver told me, during the ride back to the police station, that the woman stole away quietly on soft elephant paws, after the backswing of a broom strike meant for me clipped an officer standing behind her. Somehow, that made my trying day a little easier to bear.

By the time I reached my motel room, it was nearly 3:00 a.m. Tired and confused, the raging fire of enthusiasm that had marked the beginning of my journey had been reduced by the evening's per-plexing and frightening events to a flame the size of an oxygen-starved Bunsen burner. As I laid my yet living, breathing body down on the single bed, I took a moment to consider matters in retrospect.

First, did I or did I not see a real dead human body behind that trunk? A "no" answer would mean that I was losing either "a," my eyesight; "b," my memory; or "c," my marbles. Marbles, I could accept. However, I had just recently consulted an optometrist who assured me that my eyesight was nearly perfect. Memory? I thought back on all the dead bodies I'd seen at funeral (although none of which I was aware had a slit throat) and decided I knew what a dead body looked like. So, either I was no longer in possession of all my faculties, or I had actually seen that hideous human waste behind Great-Great-Great-Granddaddy's trunk. I concluded either possibility was valid.

Second, assuming I had seen the body, where was it now? Either it wasn't really dead and simply walked away, or it was spirited away by ghoul or ghouls unknown. Unfortunately, debate on these points was academic, at best.

The blood—which I still believed the puddles on the floor to have been—was fresh, so the murder couldn't have taken place too long before my arrival. A chill that wasn't due to ambient temperature crawled slowly up what little spine I had left. That meant the killer was probably still in the house when I arrived! Beads of cold sweat oozed from my tingling skin, as I pondered this possibility in my darkened room. But I had gone through nearly the whole house. That is, except for the basement. Was he in the basement, since I did eventually search the attic...eventually?

My eyes flew open. Of course! The attic door! I hadn't closed the attic door when I raced out of the house the first time. The killer must have absentmindedly closed it on his way out. It's a simple, natural action one might perform if one were trying to be secretive and yet in too much of a hurry to consider its appropriateness to the situation. That...that meant he was hiding in the attic all along! Whoa! Then, it was that beautiful, wonderful stone gargoyle that may have very well saved my own throat by frightening my little boy instincts into flight! I resolved right then and there that the next time I met that lovely little angel, I was going to give him, her or it a big, wet, sloppy kiss...that is, if I ever found the courage to again set foot in Hudson house.

The killer must have returned while I was fetching the police, removed the body to some concealment and replaced it with the mannequin. The blood, since it could not be completely obliterated, he wiped up as best he could and camouflaged the residue with red paint. But why hadn't Lieutenant Trevor been able to see a theory so obvious? Or was it really so obvious? After all, I hadn't told him about the fiasco with my friend, the gargoyle. Of course not. Then he'd really think I was nuts, especially after Mrs. Loudmouth's ranting and raving about my behavior. No, I think the good lieutenant would sooner have believed a politician than believe me.

Too exhausted to begin plying through Granddaddy Hudson's diary now, I slowly drifted off into that little boy land of dreams from which some of us never quite escape with visions of sugarplums strewn about my head...each one with its throat flayed wide.

# CHAPTER THREE

It was in the blackness of that empyreal world that lies somewhere beyond the border of REM to which our mind and body occasionally travel when their exhaustive states carry us too close to death. It was there that I encountered Great-Great-Great-Grandfather James Bartholomew Hudson the First. He didn't look scary, like I'd imagined a pirate should. I mean, he wasn't big and burly with unkempt hair and a long, scraggly beard. Oh, he had a beard, to be sure, and it was black, but it was close and neatly trimmed. He appeared quite dapper in his white, frilly shirt with brown pantaloons and high black boots. He wore no hat to cover his neck-length styled hair, but his wide black leather belt did sport a cutlass and two muzzle-load pistols. Despite being armed to the teeth, James the First just could not look intimidating. It was the eyes, I'm sure. An inherited Hudson trait. Kind eyes, high cheekbones and broad simile. Tough to look intimidating when you dress like a dandy and smile like a prom queen.

*I meet great, great, great Grandfather Hudson, the First*

"Who are you?" he asked in a deep, mellow voice.

"James," I replied. "James Bartholomew Hudson…the Third. Your direct descendent, some seventy-five years from now."

"Seventy-five years!"

"Give or take."

"You mean, it took seventy-five years for some land-lubbin' blowfish to figure out that second will? Seventy-five years!"

His eyes widened with wonder and dismay. When they did, I could see yet another Hudson trait that survived the generations: two differently colored eyes; one green and one blue. Perhaps I'm just sensitive to it because I see it every morning in the mirror. As I stared at him, it did seem as if I were staring into a mirror…well, except for the fact that he was something more than 130 years older than I.

"Actually," I answered, "Mom and Dad knew nothing of the second will. They lived in Des Moines. Mom's maiden name was Harrigan. She knew she had an ancestor on Grandma's side that was rumored to be a pirate, and when she married Dad, they just named me after you because they thought it was kind of neat to have a pirate for an ancestor."

His brow wrinkled. "Pirating wasn't what it's cracked up to be, boy," he said, leaning forward and looking fast into my eyes. "Did ye ever kill a man, boy?" His voice was no longer soft and mellow, but deep and cold and menacing.

My eyes were riveted to his...green to green and blue to blue. "No, sir," I answered meekly. The ice that seemed to form around his words chilled the air so much, in whatever black dimension we occupied, that my skin began to tingle.

"Well," he continued, "the first be the most difficult. Ya really doesn't know what to expect. And when ye sees the red waterfall a splashin' out his throat from ear to ear, it sort of startles ya; gets ya all queasy inside."

I really couldn't believe what I was hearing come from this rather refined-looking, well-dressed man. His eyes were dead, devoid of emotion...devoid of humanity. I began to wonder. Was it really so neat to have been named after a pirate? His eyes widened just the tiniest bit, as he spoke. "But that disappears after the first half dozen or so."

The ice had enveloped my body and my mind. I could not move. I could not speak. It was all I could do to generate a thought until he leaned back into his thronelike chair, elbows on the chair's arms and his chin resting on the fingers of his folded hands. I don't know where the words came from. Perhaps they were frozen in thought, along with my body, my mind and my heart...then released when James the First withdrew his icy gaze. "You killed him!" I blurted out, surprising even myself. His eyes widened again.

"Who?"

"Him. The dead man behind the trunk in the attic of your house...er, my house."

"I killed many a man, boy. Some with regret and some with great pleasure." He leaned forward again. "But none of them in my own home. A man's home is sacred, boy, and he can't be defiling it with blood." He rested back into his chair. "No, boy. I killed no man in my own home." He pondered a moment. "Behind the trunk, you say?"

I nodded. "The oak one with the box and the book inside."

"Oh. My diary ya found, did ya?"

I nodded again.

"Didn't yer elders ever tell ya that it's not polite to be readin' other people's private thoughts, boy?"

He was baiting me. Pirate or not, I had a mission, and he was the key that could unlock a beautiful future for me. I steeled myself. It was time for me to call his hand.

"I was only going by your instructions to the trust company you yourself hired, Grandfather."

The indignity he tried to show would have played quite well in Mrs. Willingham's eighth grade drama…but certainly not in Peoria or even Sheboygan. "I did no such thing, boy!"

"Now, Grandfather," I answered resolutely, "don't you be blowin' any smoke screens at me. I know you buried a treasure somewhere. I know you put the location in your diary in a metal box in that oak chest in your…er, my attic." His eyes narrowed again, as I continued. "And I know that, for some reason known only to yourself, you fixed it so that only the first direct descendent to bear your full name would inherit the house, the chest, the box, the diary…," I paused to let him anticipate a moment "…and the treasure."

He leaned back again, this time with an air of resignation. "Aye. The treasure," he sighed. "The curse of mankind, 'til the end of time."

"Treasure?" I asked.

He shook his head just a little, as if he were too tired or sick—or both—to muster even a tiny bit of passion. "No, boy," he uttered quietly. "Not treasure. The love of treasure. The thirst for treasure. The need of treasure. The greed."

"Human nature, Grandfather Hudson," I replied. "That hasn't changed since the dawn of time. All we did was substitute corporations and politicians for pirates and highwaymen."

He was not amused. "I'm serious, boy. The needs of greed will make a man do things unforgivable by any but God himself."

His gaze turned cold again. "Mind me, boy. If ya doesn't want to spend the better part of eternity stuck here in this no man's land… away from life…away from death…away from God himself, then keep your wits about ya and don't allow the smell of gold to make ya crazy."

I stared, chilled again by his gaze. He continued. "Promise me, boy. Swear to me on the grave of yer dear, sweet mother that you'll not give in to the greed; that your soul will stay chaste; and when the time comes, you'll do right by me." He paused to let his words bore through the ice that had formed around my brain and my soul. "Promise me, boy!" He snapped. The ice shattered from the sound of his voice, and I found my hesitant, timid voice again.

"I…I promise, Grandfather Hudson." The words trickled out of my mouth like spittle through a drunkard's lips, landing nowhere and affecting nothing.

"Like ya mean it, boy!" Grandfather screamed, his jaw in set, his eyes narrow, and the veins in his thin neck looking like a relief map of the Rocky Mountains.

"Yes, Grandfather!" I blurted out quickly. "Yes! I will do right by you! I swear it! I swear it on Mother's grave!"

He leaned back again, still serious, but calmer. "Ya see, boy, there's more here at stake than just a few trinkets of gold…much more." His chin homed in on his folded hands again, as he sank deep in thought.

"I'll tell ya, boy," he said, his eyes fixed on a spot somewhere just beyond infinity. "I'll give ya what ya needs to find the treasure. But you've got to keep your promise to me, and you've got to do me one thing first."

If I can, Grandfather," I replied in earnest. Great-Great-Great-Grandfather Hudson was back again…the man, not the pirate. His eyes were soft again, and his voice had lost the acid when he spoke.

"There's an object, a cross. It's not with the rest. It cannot be kept. It must be returned."

"Returned where, Grandfather?" I asked.

He became serious, but soft. "To its rightful place in a church, boy. A place where only the pure of heart may go."

"What church, Grandfather?"

He stared at me, his eyes sad and soft, as he spoke. "In Peru; a small village, one hundred and twenty-five leagues east of Lima."

"Peru?"

"Aye, boy. The book will tell you where. The book will tell you everything. You have to do this for me, boy. You have to do it first before you can find the rest of the treasure."

"But Peru, Grandfather?" I argued. "I know nothing of Peru. Why, I've never been out of the country."

He leaned a serious face forward. "You have no choice, boy."

I matched him; green to green and blue to blue. "I have no *money*, Grandfather."

He smiled and settled back again. "I thought of that, boy," he said with a slight smirk. "Did that just before I...I...I died." His mind and his voice trailed off together into space again, like two lovers disappearing hand in hand into a mist. "Ya know, boy. Kind of funny bein' dead, it is...if that's what I am. I don't know...here."

"Just where are we, Grandfather?" I asked quietly.

"I don't rightly know, boy," he answered, his voice dropping to just above a whisper. "I been here since the day I died."

"Why, Grandfather?" I asked, with the innocent curiosity of a six year old who can't understand why his pet hamster died.

Grandfather Hudson became serious again. "I cannot say. I cannot." He paused a moment. "Our time here together grows short, boy, so listen well." We again leaned in together. He spoke softly, quietly, as if he were afeared of being overheard. "The secret to finding the cross ye'll find on these pages." He spoke now—slowly, deliberately. "Five...fifty-three...eighty-seven...six." He let that sink in just a moment. "Got that, boy? Five, fifty-three, eighty-seven, six... in that order. Ya can't be mixin' 'em up, boy. They won't work any other way." He paused again and then repeated. "Five, fifty-three, eighty-seven, six."

I searched amid the clutter of my befuddled brain to find four empty cells in which to store these numeric nuggets of gold. "Five." I began mentally opening the door to each locked brain cell and sealing the golden nuggets inside. "Fifty-three." *Clank!* The door shut on the second. "Eighty-seven." *Wham!* That one slammed so hard my teeth rattled. And finally, "six." Wait! It got away! I lunged at the fleeing digit, catching it just by the bottom curl, like a football linebacker on a shoestring tackle. "Six," I said again, as I wrestled the squirming fugitive into its brain cell and slammed the door shut.

Great-Great-Great-Grandfather Hudson stared silently...not moving, not blinking and not even breathing, as if he could see my struggles to lock each number away (of course, he was already dead; and this was just a dream, so I assumed breathing was optional). When the last cell door slammed shut, he paused just a bit and then spoke, "Got it, boy?"

"Yes, sir, Grandfather," I replied. "I got it."

He continued. "Good. Now, on each of those pages, ye'll find hidden directions. I did that so no land lubbin' skunk could steal it away."

"Hidden, Grandfather? But couldn't just anybody read it?"

"Aye, boy." He nodded. "But they won't have the key."

"The key? The key to what?"

He looked slightly irritated. "The numbers, boy! The numbers. Them's yer key to everything. Read it close, boy. Study them well and know 'em by heart. Use them more than once, if the need be."

"Grandfather Hudson," I answered, gently shaking my head, "I just don't know..."

"Silence, boy!" he snapped, his eyes shooting fire. "There is no time for doubt! There is no time!" His voice grew softer, but no less intense, and his eyes showed a fear that only the condemned could know. "There...is...no...*time*."

"Yes. Yes, Grandfather," I stammered for the first time with a genuine fright.

After an eternity of silence, he spoke again. "On each of those pages, ye'll find a clue to the next step. Use the numbers, if you run adrift." He paused and thought a moment. "Now, have ye found my portrait, boy?"

"Portrait?" I wondered. "No, I haven't."

"Well then," he continued. "Just off the library room in my house is a small office. Hanging behind the desk is a portrait I had commissioned before I died. Study it well."

"But why, Grandfather?" I asked, my brain muddled with mush from this long day's madness. "What am I looking for?" Scarcely had those words passed my lips, then Grandfather impulsively jerked upright, as if hit by a lightning bolt. His face went pale, and his eyes lost their luster. With a very loud bang, the chair on which he sat began to rock about wildly and rise into the black nothingness that surrounded us.

"Grandfather!" I cried, as I tried to reach for him. "Grandfather! What's happening?" But my words were lost, and my muscles were locked in tight. I could only scream with all my might.

His pleas grew faint, as this apparition that was Great-Great-Great-Grandfather James Bartholomew Hudson the First began to return to the elements from which we all had come, atom by sparkling atom. "Stay pure of heart, boy! Pure of heart! Only those pure of heart can succeed! Don't let the greed consume your heart, boy! Take the cross back! The cross, boy! The cross! Promise me ye'll take it back, boy! Promise me, boy!"

"I promise, Grandfather!" I cried, tears rising up through my throat to my eyes from some long-forgotten boyhood well we choose, in our refined adulthood, to cap off. "I promise!"

As his essence disappeared into yesteryear, I couldn't quite catch his last few words before he was gone. But I was gone also. That is, my surroundings were no longer a mystery. I jerked upright in the bed, my eyes snapping open, just in time to see the last beams of light from the hallway die behind the closing of my motel room door. Or did I?

Was this, perhaps, just part of the same fantastic illusion from which I had just escaped? Muffled footsteps running down the hallway answered that question. Then, someone really had been in my room, while my exhausted body was attempting to rejuvenate itself. But who? Why? My heart froze in midbeat. The book!

As a proverbial wild man from Borneo, as a madman possessed of demons, as a man whose future had just disappeared down the tufted hall of a cheap motel, a cry that began somewhere in the secret chamber of my Neanderthal ancestry vomited into the stillness of the night.

"NOOOOO!" I screamed, as I bolted from the bed, bounced off the old, upright dresser and slammed my hand into the light switch on the wall. Gone! The book was gone! I had carelessly laid my future, my life on a cheap, laminated coffee table that accented nothing in the room!

Not usually given to expletives, I can't really remember the exact words and phrases that were escaping my lips to express the shock, anger, frustration and fear I felt at my loss. But I do know their volume and intensity were considerable. So much so that hardly had the last echo bounced down the bare walls of the hallway outside, then the room phone rang. It was the night manager, asking about my plight, telling me I was waking the other guests and demanding I quiet down, which I did not. I just kept yelling to him that someone had stolen my book and my life, and demanding that he call the police to catch the thief. I remember yelling, "Stop him! Stop him!" Then, I threw the phone receiver down and raced out the door to catch the culprit myself.

Now, being as yet unmarried and without children, and having lived contentedly alone for a number of years, and my parents having been as open-minded as they were, I have come to find it healthy and agreeable to sleep...well, in the nude, without clothes, naked, as it were. This is a fact that, given my hysterical frenzy to retrieve Grandfather Hudson's diary, went unnoticed by me. This condition did not, however, escape the attention of those several motel patrons of all ages and both sexes who, hearing the commotion I had created, peered out their doors to see a stark naked, raving maniac running down the hallway, screaming for some unseen, imaginary thief to stop.

Thus, it was that I enjoyed, for the second time in less than eight hours, the gracious hospitality of Lieutenant Trevor's jail.

# CHAPTER FOUR

It was hard to tell if Lieutenant Trevor was grinning, grimacing, growling or gaseous. The veins on his neck stood prominent, but the corners of his wide mouth were drawn up a remarkable distance toward each ear. His eyes became slits, and his white pearlies clenched together tightly, like the jaws of a tenacious Badger.

"Mis-ter Hudson," he began very slowly, in a voice that wavered with anger. "Did...you...not...understand...what I said last night?"

"Well, sir," I answered, "I wasn't speeding."

He came nose to ear with me. "You...were...NAKED!" he screamed. "In a motel parking lot! On a street across from a playground!"

Whether it was due to the force of his words or the intensity of the cheese and garlic he had for lunch, my head snapped away, banging into the back of the chair on which I sat. He stood erect again, hands on hips like a young father who caught his prodigal son with a hand in the cookie jar.

"Well," I said meekly, "that was kind of an accident."

"An accident."

"Yes, sir." I hesitated. "You see, I usually sleep in the nude."

"Naked? Well, I suppose a lot of people do that, but they don't usually jump out of bed and go running down the motel hallway and out into the parking lot!"

"Yes, well, that's the rest of the story."

"OK, Paul Harvey, lay it on me."

I then proceeded to relate to Trevor the story of how I found the book inside the trunk before being frightened by the dead mannequin in the attic and how I dreamed about Great-Great-Great-Grandfather Hudson that night and being awakened by a loud bang, just in time to see the room door closing and hear footsteps running down the hall. I did not, however, elaborate to Trevor the details of my conversation with Grandfather Hudson, partly because I was wary of trusting anybody—even a cop—but mostly because I wasn't really sure even I believed it. I mean, come on. Getting directions to a fabulous treasure from a dead pirate in a dream? Let's get real here.

I explained to Trevor, or tried to anyway, just how distraught I was about the robbery and how valuable a keepsake that diary was. I figured he bought it because after I squirmed and pleaded and came close to tears, he gave me another warning about acting impulsively and then said he'd put a couple of men on the case. My admiration for this lawman's insight and understanding was growing.

"I'll get a squad to take you back to your motel. He can canvass the floor to see if anybody else saw or heard this phantom book thief," Trevor said, as we walked toward the door. "And while he's doing that, you can change clothes and give us back our uniform."

I looked down at the bright orange jail jumpsuit they had given me to wear. "Oh, I don't know," I answered in a futile attempt at some gallows humor. "It kind of accents my eyes." He was not amused.

On the way back to the motel, I asked the driver, an affable officer with a jolly disposition that would have served him well as a department store Santa Claus, how long he'd known Lieutenant Trevor.

"Not long," he answered. "He came from out of state a couple years ago. Took the department by storm, he did. Wasn't long at all 'til he had bars on his collars."

"Quite a go-getter, huh?"

"Well, there's some that say he had inside help from somebody on the Safety Commission Board. But I don't really believe that. Pretty smart cookie, he is."

"Think he can find my book?"

"Is a bear Catholic?" the officer asked, with a grin that cried out for thunderous applause.

"Huh?" His answer gave me pause. I thought a moment and then smiled. "Oh, yes. Of course," I answered. "Good one." Dry sense of humor this Officer Santa Claus has. "Is there a bank in town?" I asked.

"Yes, *a* bank…as in, one; meaning less than two, but more than zero." His reply came rapidly. "It's pretty much on our way. I'll show you where it is, but don't rob it today. I'd say you've seen enough of our jail."

"Couldn't agree more." I chuckled. "What about a library?"

"Practically right across the street."

To that end, he was true. We did detour to the left, about five blocks from the motel. There on the right was a small bank. Judging by the architecture, I would say that it had been around long enough for Jesse James to have robbed it at least twice. On the opposite corner was a modern-looking building that housed the town's library.

"Is that the main library?" I asked.

"Yup," he answered. "There's two branches. One on either side of town."

One bank and three libraries. I'd say this town has its priorities straight.

"Hey, look," I asked, as we entered the motel parking lot, the one wherein I had allowed my true and unabashed self to be seen by everyone. "Would you mind coming to the desk with me and verifying that I am not an escaped fugitive from your jail? When I ran out of my room this morning, I didn't have a lot of pockets I could stuff my room key into."

This brought a hearty laugh from Officer Santa Claus. His round little belly did, indeed, shake like a bowl full of jelly.

"Great. You'll get to meet Iris, the owner's wife. She manages the place while her husband's away."

"Away? What does he do?"

"Runs a charter boat," Santa replied. "Not a lot of business this time of year, but he makes do." He parked the car, and we headed into the office.

Iris was a lady approaching middle age, of enchanting proportions and delightful disposition.

"Mornin', Iris," my jolly escort offered.

She stopped sorting mail and looked up from behind the worn registration desk, her eyes riveted on my jailhouse attire.

"Mornin', Chris." She hesitated slightly, just long enough for my mind to rail at her words. Chris? Chris? This jolly fat man, who looked like he spends every December 24 staring at the north end of southbound reindeer? His name is Chris? That was just too ironic. I thought it fortunate she hadn't called him Mr. Kringle. That surely would have sent me screaming into the street in search of a passing bus to end my misery.

"Mister Hudson?" Iris's words snapped me back to a reality just slightly less bizarre than the one I'd imagined. "Mister Hudson, I'm sorry. I guess I didn't recognize you with... with...uh...."

"With jail clothes on?" I suggested.

"Well...with *any* clothes on!" she roared out loud in boisterous laughter. Officer Santa Claus slammed his hand down on the counter and joined her choruses of chortles, chuckles, giggles and guffaws at my expense.

When they were exhausted, she looked at me again, her lovely brown eyes soothing any ire I may have harbored. "I'm sorry, Mister Hudson," she went on. "But nobody was hurt, and you have to admit it was...was...*funny*. Downright hilarious. One for the books." She paused just an instant. "But at least there were no children on the playground, so they're not going to charge you with indecent exposure." She grinned again. "Or should I say...*decent* exposure?"

With that, Officer Kringle proceeded to bust the other gut laughing. Iris became infected and joined him. Thankfully, this spell subsided.

"Really, Mister Hudson," Iris added. "You should consider joining a health club. Those love handles are getting a little too handy." Again, with the hilarity. I wasn't sure how much of this fun I could stand. "Of course," she went on, "it does cover up that appendectomy scar."

"Will it ever end?" my mind screamed.

"That was gall bladder, madam, not appendectomy," I said flatly, my patience wearing somewhat thin. "Appendectomy is on the right side. Gall bladder is on the left." Wait a minute! How did she know? I wondered if she had witnessed my degradation. But managers rarely work the night shift.

"Excuse me," I butted in. "How did you know about my surgery? Were you here last night?"

She stopped laughing and pointed to a security camera. "We got 'em all over the place."

Duh! Color me stupid. Why hadn't I thought of that before? Why hadn't Trevor confiscated the tapes already? "Does Lieutenant Trevor know about those tapes?" I asked. Barely had the words cleared my lips when Officer Kringle's radio began to squawk.

"Dispatch, three-five. Dispatch, three-five."

Santa fumbled for the radio on his belt. "Three-five. Go ahead."

The voice on the other end was flat, calm and nearly expressionless, as befits someone whose job it is to keep everybody else calm. "One-five was wondering if you could get the surveillance tapes for the last twenty-four hours from the motel. Over."

"Roger," Kringle replied. "Will do."

"Thank you. Dispatch out."

"Three-five out."

Iris grinned again and reached under the counter. "Kind of thought he might want these," she said, plopping two VHS cassettes on the top. "Way ahead of him."

Santa reached over to pick them up.

"But," she cautioned, "I can't guarantee their quality. The system we got is so cheap, you really can't see much." She chuckled. "Well, except maybe for an occasional appendectomy scar."

"Gall bladder!" I blurted out. "Gall bladder!"

"Whatever."

Officer Santa Claus picked up the worn boxes, tucked them under his arm and turned to leave.

"I think one of the cameras got a short in it somewhere. Keeps cuttin' in and out," Iris called after him.

"OK," was all Kringle said, as he waddled through the door into a rising sun.

I turned to this comely creature with the soft eyes and sharp wit. "Excuse me," I asked, "but could I get a spare key for my room, please…just long enough to change out of this Halloween costume."

She chuckled as she handed me another room key. "I guess you do sort of look like a fugitive from the pumpkin patch. Here ya go. You can drop it back by the next time you…" She stopped abruptly, a look of pity emanating from her eyes. "Well, never mind. I guess we beat that one to death."

"Thank you," I replied. "I think we have."

While warm water in the shower dissipated the tension that had trussed me up like a Thanksgiving turkey, my mind once again pondered upon the day's events. First, I really did have Great-Great-Great-Grandfather Hudson's diary. It was real. Not a figment of my imagination. I did lay it on the coffee table in the room before my exhausted mind wandered into never-never land to meet with Grandfather Hudson. Fact. It was there when I went to sleep and gone when I woke up. So *somebody* had to have come in, stole the book and slipped out again just before I woke up. Then, maybe my dream about meeting Grandfather Hudson really was just that…a dream. And the noise of Grandfather Hudson's chair was really the thief tripping over a chair or table leg. Maybe.

When I finally forced myself out of that warm, relaxing shower, I thought I'd better call Trevor's office to see when the tapes might be reviewed. The desk sergeant said Trevor had already gone for the day, but he'd be back for the night shift at about midnight. All right. That would give me enough time to pursue other twists in this aberrant enigma. First, I would check at the bank to see if Grandfather Hudson really had left a bundle of cash for his namesake. Then, on to the library to dig up what I could on Grandfather and try to find out, sans assistance from his waylaid diary, anything I could about unfound treasures that might fit his time period. Daunting tasks indeed for a substitute school teacher and part-time custodial engineer from the cornfields around Des Moines.

I, who once catered a fine and tasty (if somewhat used) lunch to thousands of grateful fish, while crossing the vast expanse (maybe two miles) of Saylorville Lake near Des Moines, in a twenty-five-foot chartered fishing cruiser, on a calm and sunny day, was going to retrace the voyage of my wayward but strangely loveable great-great-great-grandfather to the some whereabouts of a fabulous treasure and then return a jewel-encrusted cross to a remote church somewhere east of Lima, Peru, so that his tortured soul will finally be at peace. *I* was going to do this…somehow, not anybody else, not John Paul Jones, not Admiral Perry, not even Johnny Quest or Hadji. Just me.

As I sank slowly onto one of the mismatched chairs near that cursed black hole called a coffee table, the proverbial wet mackerel with the acrid aroma of reality slapped me right upside the head. And as my eyes glazed over, my mouth began to utter what my left brain had been trying to tell me all along.

"How in the he…"

*BAM! BAM! BAM! BAM! BAM!*

"Aghhhh!" My scream startled me almost as much as the pounding on my door.

"Mister Hudson," came the commanding voice of Officer Kringle. "Mister Hudson, are you in there? Open the door, please."

My first impulse to immediately obey the orders of a duly sworn officer of the law was thankfully thwarted by the pain in my left middle toe, as it made clumsy contact with the leg of that blasted coffee table. Again, a momentary lapse in civility flowed from my lips and made an indelible impression in space and time.

"Mister Hudson," Kringle asked with genuine concern, "are you all right?"

Looking down at my injured toe made me realize that I was again about to open my door to the world…au naturel. That would have surely sealed my fate as a weirdo, a troublemaker and a pervert in this quiet little coastal community.

"Yes. Of course. I'm all right," I called quickly. "Just let me put on my robe. I just got out of the shower."

Putting on my robe, I cinched the belt as tightly as I could around my stomach and double knotted it. How paranoid we humans are…at least, some of us. I thought now of how a horse must feel when getting saddled and felt a strange bond with the poor beast.

Officer Kringle's grinning Santa Claus face greeted me as I opened the door; it completely belied the booming command voice he had used.

"Mister Hudson," he said politely, "I forgot to pick up the orange jumpsuit to bring back to the jail. Could I get it now, please?"

"Oh, of course," I answered, turning back into the room to retrieve the garment. "Actually, I was hoping to keep it as a souvenir."

"A reminder of what not to do?"

"Yes. Something like that."

He turned to go and then stopped. "Oh, by the way," he added. "I checked the hotel register, and two out of the other three guests in this wing last night have already left. But we can get a hold of them if we have to; that is, assuming they gave their right names and addresses." He winked, as if I were supposed to be shocked that this rundown fugitive-from-skid-row motel could be used as a sanctuary for illicit love affairs.

"What about the third?" I asked.

"Oh. He's a permanent resident. Half-blind, half-deaf and alcoholic."

"Well, did you talk to him?"

"Sure, but he said he passed out about midnight and didn't wake up until about ten this morning. Not much help, I'm afraid."

Sweet. No book, no suspect, no witnesses…and maybe no video. Things were just rolling right along. I could only hope the video might be useable, and I could track down information on Grandfather Hudson at the library. But first, breakfast and a visit to the bank.

# CHAPTER FIVE

A master criminal, I ain't. Nor could I ever be, especially in a town this size. News travels fast in a small town; bad news, like wildfire. Between the mudpack monster outside my house last night, Officer Santa Claus and the charmingly cheeky Iris, I was sure my indiscretions were the lead story on every tongue-wagging lip in town.

As I entered the little seaside café, appropriately named The Jolly Roger, I felt every eye touch my body somewhere. They knew. They all knew, even the kids, barely out of the high chair and into a big kid's booster seat. Even they knew about the stranger in town; the crazy man who prowled a haunted house at midnight laughed and cried maniacally beneath a full Halloween moon, drove like a madman down the streets of this sleepy little town, screaming bloody murder; and finally, bared his soul—and everything else—to the world by bolting out a motel door to run willy-nilly naked around the parking lot. Oh, yes. They all knew.

I found the only table open and sat down. My gaze traveled to each patron in sight. I was sure Lieutenant Trevor had stopped here on his way home and, in a fatigue-induced lapse of proper police protocol, spilled his guts to an awestruck audience. This was undoubtedly followed by the comic and comely Iris, who I'm sure just couldn't wait for lunchtime to titillate her friends with tales of my Lady Godiva impression, right down to my appendectomy scar… and all in its proximity. Her laughter bounced off the inner walls of my befuddled mind, like the mocking of a lovers' quarrel.

"Appendectomy scar! Ha!" The sound of her laughter echoed in my head and nibbled at the bindings of my self-control, something I've been losing far too often lately. Finally, they snapped.

"Gall bladder! Gall bladder, damn it! Gall bladder!" My words flew out like frightened starlings.

"Excuse me, sir?" It was the dainty, somewhat apprehensive voice of my young waitress. I looked at the poor girl, her eyes wide, and her cherub cheeks skewed in confusion. I had to think fast.

"Oh," I stammered. "Uh...uh, excuse me. I was just thinking out loud. I, uh...I'm doing a play back home...in Des Moines. I play a doctor...a surgeon. I guess I was absentmindedly rehearsing out loud. I'm really sorry."

"I see," came the unconvincing reply. "Well, would you like coffee?" She placed a menu down in front of me.

"Yes, please. Are you still serving breakfast?"

"All day."

"Great. I'll have a short stack of pancakes, two eggs over easy, sausage links, and a large milk, please."

"Coming right up." She smiled. Her pasty demeanor was vaguely reminiscent of a float queen greeting her subjects, lacking only the automatonlike actions of the arm, elbow, and wrist in the obligatory wave, as she turned about and surveyed each coffee cup at each table, on her way back to the kitchen. The previous occupants at my table must have left just prior to my arrival, since it was lacking utensils, water glasses, or even placemats.

Feeling quite self-conscious, I was grateful when the float queen brought my coffee along with the necessary hardware and a colorful placemat, decorated with puzzles, games and interesting pirate facts on one side, and a map of the area on the reverse. Good idea. I decided to set the placemat aside and use the map in my travels around town. It had the flavor of an old sailing chart and seemed to cover mostly the seaside area for about five miles on either side of the town. Little Jolly Roger flags pointed out historical markers and tourist traps. Nice touch, I thought.

Presently, my breakfast arrived, and I abandoned my cartographer studies for more mundane things...like the food my starving body was craving. Funny how, during times of intensity, the body can't make the brain understand that it also has needs until the crises have passed. Then it's pirates and plunder be damned…I'm *hungry*!

Poor things. The overcooked eggs and undercooked pancakes had not the proverbial prayer. Down they went! I resolved to be more gentle and civil with my sausage links. To help with this honorable resolution, I began musing over the kiddie games and other scribblings on the opposite side of the placemat. On one of them, I successfully navigated a maze to get Captain Kidd back to London. I wondered if whoever made this knew the unfortunate pirate would be hanged once he got there. My guess is not.

What appeared to be a small poem or limerick caught my eye. As I read its verses, my mouth kept chewing, but my mind froze in place. My eyes became wide as the yolks in my eggs. This is what the limerick said:

"There once was a pirate named James
Who, for stealing gold, everyone blames
To find the loot that he took
You must first find the book
Before it goes up high in flames.

If you are now quite perplexed
Be there on Saturday, next
Be where, you might say?
Slip four, Emerald Bay
At midnight, to save James's text."

The shock sent shivers up and down my spine. Scientists say that it takes a total of twenty-two muscles in coordinated symphonic effort to swallow one's food. Needless to say, this shock to my brain caused several off-key clinkers in this symphony, and I suddenly began choking, coughing and hacking…all those things one does when food and drink get sucked into the lungs. Immediately, my waitress and several patrons rushed to my rescue. Two muscular men who had been at the next table quickly bent me over and began pounding on my back to dislodge the errant morsels from my windpipe. That worked, although I wasn't sure later which hurt more, the food in my trachea or the bruises on my back. Logically, I would say the former, but it didn't seem so at the time.

As it is sometimes with persons in stressful situations, my subconscious reasoned that I must, at all costs, hold on to that placemat, which I did, even when getting mercifully pummeled by two large men, whom I suspected could have or did play linebacker for the Chicago Bears. When I had sufficiently recovered, I thanked them very much for their quick response and sat back down at my table, taking small sips of water to soothe my sore throat and wash any leftover morsels down. After the gentlemen returned to their table, I turned the map back over and found Emerald Bay about three miles up the coast. Deciding I was no longer hungry, I folded the placemat in quarters and clutched it tightly, as I got up to pay my bill. Several tables had emptied out and a busboy was clearing them off.

The concept of luck in my life had mostly eluded me...at least, good luck. I have often quipped that, with my luck, I could come in second place in a one-horse race...and then find out I was beaten by a mule. The café was small, its tables and booths in close proximity to each other; much too close, I would say. With wallet in one hand and placemat in the other, I threaded my way through the maze toward the register counter. As a boy, I was never coordinated enough to play basketball; somehow, the ball, my hands and my feet all operated independently. However, that day, I was to run into the one person who could out clumsy me...quite literally. Tall, gangly and sporting feet the size of water walkers, the lad picked up a large pan piled high with dirty dishes, food scraps, and placemats in various stages of soiledness and turned directly into my path, one of his size 12s landing on top of my pitiful size 9½ D. The rest of my body finding my foot unable to move to its new location on the floor, did so itself, accompanied by a veritable garbage dump of dishes, food, and placemats.

Again, I had a crowd of rescuers around me, asking me if I were all right. Had I broken anything? Did I need help getting up? Indeed, I had not broken anything; at least, that I could tell then.

I had caught myself on the edge of a nearby table and was able to soften my contact with the hardwood floor. I was, however, covered in a mixture of meals that would drive any foraging pack of garbage rats to distraction. Actually, reflecting on it later, the aroma wasn't all that displeasing, and I thought that analysis of its individual parts might yield a tasty new type of dish…or terminal heartburn; I wasn't sure which.

Pulling myself up from the floor, I assured my benevolent onlookers that I was physically fine and only my dignity, or what little was left of it, was injured. The waitress and the café's chef were apologetic in the extreme, the chef saying that the young offending oaf would soon find himself digging through the dumpsters for meals. I looked around for the unfortunate lad. He had apparently panicked and bolted out the back door. Recalling my own youth of about that age, I implored them not to take any action against the boy. After all, accidents do happen, especially at that age. The float queen dove in with a towel to wipe the mess from my trousers, then a wave of modesty induced her to hand the towel to me. As I finished wiping myself off, I realized my placemat, my map, the only tangible clue I had to find Grandfather Hudson's diary was not in my hand! Panic struck.

"My map," I said, trying not to show my alarm. "The placemat I had. There was a map on it that would be very useful in finding my way around your lovely city. Did anybody pick it up?"

"Oh, we've got plenty of them," the chef replied.

"Yes. But I had nearly finished one of the crossword puzzles on it, and I'd hate to have to start over again." I lied, but this was war.

"Oh, here it is," said the float queen, picking up an odorous paper that was folded over twice and dripping with spaghetti sauce.

I latched on to it as if it were gold, which it was, in a manner of speaking. "Thank you so much," I said. "Now, if I may just pay my check and be on my way, I need to change into something a little less…culinary."

"Oh no, sir!" the chef exclaimed. "No charge at all. The meal is on the house. Please accept that as our gratitude for your understanding and patience. Please. I insist."

"Well, that's not necessary, but thank you. Thank you very much." The cherub queen brought a small plastic bag in which to put my placemat. Stuffing it in, I again thanked them for their kindness and exited to my car.

Back in my motel room, I showered and put my sticky, stinky wardrobe into a bag provided by the laundry service. Ordinarily, I would be too frugal to utilize a laundry service, but these were not ordinary times, and I had much yet to accomplish this day. After dressing, I decided to double check the information on the placemat and scour it for anything I may have missed the first time. I thought the best course of action would be bringing it to Lieutenant Trevor. He could follow me to Emerald Bay and apprehend the culprit who had stolen Grandfather's diary. Pulling it out of the bag, I laid the placemat on that accursed coffee table and wiped off the stains. Thank goodness it was made of heavy weight paper with a light coating of plastic (I assumed). The spaghetti sauce mixed with orange juice and strawberry preserves wiped off fairly easily. I resisted the perverted temptation to taste the mixture and see what new flavor experience I might find, figuring that an ambulance ride to the hospital would certainly mean the coup d'état of my expedition.

Opening the placemat up, I scoured it closely. There, down in the corner, was the limerick.

"There once was a pirate named Kidd
And everyone knew what he did
In a move that was bold
He stole the king's gold
And..."

Wait a minute! That's not what my placemat said. It's gone. The float queen must have picked up the wrong placemat. Curse the luck! But was it luck? First, there was only one table open at the café. Then, there were no placemats on it. Thirdly, the limerick was specific to my situation. That is, it mentioned Grandfather, the treasure, and the diary. But the key was the meeting at slip four, Emerald Bay, at midnight on Saturday, next. Let's see, that was two days away.

That would be the confirmation. For nobody would send hundreds or even thousands of tourists on a wild goose chase in the middle of the night by printing such a thing on every placemat…would they?

I debated whether I should bring this up to Lieutenant Trevor now. I mean, he already must think I'm three fries shy of a happy meal. All the bizarre things that had happened to me—that only I knew for sure really did…I think. My word. I was even doubting myself now. Des Moines sure was looking good to me. I thought maybe the best course of action would be to return to the café and recheck the placemats. But first, I needed to get to the bank before it closed and then to the library. Turning the plastic bag inside out, I wiped off what was now the outside, stuffed the map into it and headed out the motel door fully clothed.

My initial suspicions about the age of the bank seemed accurate, as I stared at its massive brown stones, barred antique windows and huge steel doors. I thought that even Grandfather Hudson would have had a tough time robbing this one. As I learned later, this was only the second structure the bank had occupied in nearly two hundred years. I entered. The structure's interior definitely outpaced the exterior. The floor was highly polished hardwood accented by ornate area rugs on which rested overstuffed arm chairs, cherry wood tables, and floor lamps that resembled gaslights. I didn't even cringe at the overused phrase, "stepping back in time." There were only two or three patrons at the two teller stations framed by ornate wooden archways. Again, every eye seemed to be on me, crawling all over my skin, as I approached a middle-aged teller. Her graying hair was in a bun, topping a round, slightly wrinkled face, with wide-set, kind eyes. The blue high-collar dress she wore buttoned up the front with large, round, cloth-covered buttons and frilly cuffs. Maybe I really had been transported back to 1900.

"Excuse me, madam. May I speak with a bank executive, please?" She stared at me a moment.

"Oh, yes, sir, Mister Hudson. Right away." She locked her cash drawer and disappeared through an office door. Confirmation! I knew then that I was a celebrity. I had achieved star status. I chuckled, wondering if they had a Walk of Fame and a star with my name on it, around which I could make impressions of my hands and feet for the edification and enlightenment of all future generations. My amusement was all-consuming.

"Mister Hudson." The man's voice was high and soft. It gently pulled my consciousness back to reality. He was short, thin and balding with eyes that appeared very kind; or perhaps it was the softness of his voice that just made them seem so. He grabbed my hand and shook it with animated motions, as if he were greeting a best friend from his childhood long lost. "We have been waiting for you, sir," he continued. "You've been quite the talk of the town, since we received word that you had been located." I noted that he, too, was dressed for the preceding century, wearing a dark pin-striped suit with wide lapels and a matching vest. From one of the buttons on the vest hung a gold watch chain with a fob in the shape of a typewriter, the watch being placed upright in the left vest pocket.

"So it appears," I answered. "Mister Jasper, I presume." There was a short, awkward pause.

The statement had apparently caught the man off guard. The teller's eyes widened a little.

"Uh...no. My name is Farington. Aloysius Farington. I'm the bank president. Uh...Mister Jasper is...uh, no longer with us. He... uh, he was made an offer he couldn't refuse."

"Oh," I answered. "Going up in the world, huh?"

"I certainly hope so," replied the teller, rolling her green eyes around in their makeup-plastered sockets. Farington shot her an unmistakable go-back-to-work look. Without another word, she wheeled about and returned to her cage.

"Please, Mister Hudson," Farington said. "Let's go into my office, and you can tell me why you're here."

"Well," I said, as we walked toward the old office door with the frosted window. "I'm sure you know why I'm here. My presence certainly hasn't been much of a secret."

He gave a knowing chuckle. "Yes, so I understand."

I could swear I had seen Farington's office in an old black-and-white Hollywood sailing movie from the oak roll-top desk to the padded oak captain's chairs. The walls above the wainscoting displayed portraits of bankers, sea captains, and sailing industry moguls dressed in an array of period business suits and uniforms that could have easily come out of a theater major's costuming guide. Many of the men sported beards, handlebar moustaches, and mutton chops. What a history major's delight! I fully expected a full-length portrait of President Ulysses Simpson Grant to occupy the honor spot instead of James Earl Carter. Nestled in the center of this richly appointed room was a marble pedestal on which sat the most exquisitely detailed replica of a clipper ship I had ever seen. I couldn't hide my amazement.

"Wow!" I exclaimed, with the delight of a schoolboy on Christmas morning.

"That's the *Rainbow*. First clipper ship ever built. My great-great-great-grandfather was the purser aboard her. She sailed out of San Francisco one morning in 1866 and was never heard from again."

"No clues?"

"Nope. Not so much as a floating skiff."

"Lost in a storm, perhaps?"

His eyebrows narrowed slightly, in doubt. "Perhaps. She wouldn't have been the first to go down without a trace." He hesitated. "Some say it was pirates."

"Pirates? I thought piracy was pretty much eradicated by then."

"Almost. But then, 'almost' only counts in horseshoes and hand grenades."

He pushed three buttons near the corner of the desk. Three small screens, located a couple inches inside what looked like old-fashioned pigeon holes, brightened up. One showed the bank lobby and the other two, entrances.

"Very creative," I offered. "I'm impressed."

"There are more, but they are classified. Security, you know."

"Understood. That's actually quite comforting."

A self-satisfied look came over him. "Thank you." He paused. "Now, as to your great-great-great-grandfather's account...." He unlocked a desk drawer and pulled out a manila file folder. "Before we begin, I do need to see two forms of identification and the original letter signed by Mister Jasper."

"Oh, of course," I said, pulling out my wallet and the folded envelope I had received from the trust company's former employee. "Right here." I handed him my driver's license, a credit card, and the envelope.

After being satisfied that none was counterfeit, he opened the file and laid it out between us. The top page was printed. On it was listed an inventory of the gold and precious jewels that Grandfather Hudson had left for his namesake along with the current estimated value of each item.

"As you can see, your ancestor apparently did not believe in paper currency," Farington said.

"Nor do I blame him." I smiled.

He chuckled. "Neither do I, but I guess we're stuck with it now." He used the long "i" sound in "neither," befitting his formal appearance. "Now, according to your ancestor's wishes, we have had the value of these items appraised every five years, except in the event a rightful heir is located, it would be done immediately, which it was about a month ago. The same firm has done it every time for the last...well, hundred years or so." He leaned back in the ornate, padded office chair to allow me space for examining the list. "However," he went on, "if you'd prefer to have it independently appraised, we would certainly understand."

I'm sure he watched my different-colored eyeballs all but pop out from their sockets, as I perused the list of "trinkets" Grandfather Hudson had left me. Farington's words finally broke through my wall of amazement. "Uh...no," I stammered. "That won't be necessary. I'm sure it's reasonable. Perhaps at a later time."

He was silent as I thumbed through the stack of papers. It was a virtual museum for the evolution of bean-counting technology. The bottom page, being carefully hand-lettered on paper yellowed with age, was followed with progressive innovations in record keeping from early typewriters with uneven keystrokes, all the way up to the newest electric printing machines. But it was the bottom line on the top page that took my breath away. I tried not to stutter.

"Five hundred, twenty-seven thousand, six hundred twelve dollars...and eighteen cents." I cleared my throat of its obstruction...

that being my heart, and continued. "Well, that seems like a tidy sum to start with."

Somewhat amused, Farington drew closer. "Not including, mind you, that magnificent house, which is appraised at just under four hundred thousand dollars. Which brings the grand total of your inheritance to just under a million dollars…minus applicable fees, of course."

"Of course," I said, in my best business voice. "Could I see these items now, please?"

"Certainly," he answered, pushing yet another magic button on his state-of-the-art antique. A soft female voice emanated from somewhere in one of the pigeon holes. I wondered if a soft, gentle voice was a prerequisite for working here. Pleasant anyway.

"Yes, Mister Farington?"

"Mister Hudson needs access to his safe-deposit box. Could you get the forms ready, please?"

"Yes, sir. Right away."

Farington leaned back in his chair again. "Not to pry, Mister Hudson, but have you thought much about what you're going to do now? I mean, you own a magnificent home now and have a substantial sum to help you get a leg up on life. Have you given any thought to settling down here?"

I hesitated, thinking. He apparently took that as disapproval of his question, adding quickly, "I hope I'm not out of line here, but if you were thinking of staying, there are many ways the bank could help you get settled."

"No, not out of line at all, Mister Farington. I appreciate your concern," I assured him. "I am looking at that possibility, but it's much too soon to be making big decisions like that."

"Of course. Well, whatever you decide, the bank will always be here to help."

"Thank you, sir." I hesitated again. "Uh, I do have a one question, though."

"You may fire when ready, Gridley."

Ah! A history buff, this soft-spoken bank manager is, I thought, to have quoted this famously understated line. I decided to match him up. "Commodore George Dewey, spoken to the commander of his flagship to kick off the Spanish-American War of 1898, in Manila Bay."

His eyes widened. "Yes. Aboard the USS *Olympia*. I'm impressed, Mister Hudson."

"Thank you, sir. I teach history classes whenever they need a substitute."

"What's your question?"

"Money, sir. I have all this wealth and no money. Well, that is except for my accounts back in Des Moines. But I may need a fair amount of capital to accomplish what I must here. I can open an account here, but that would take some time."

He smiled. "Not a problem, Mister Hudson. We'll extend a line of credit based on some of the items on your list. Then, we'll have the funds transferred to your bank in Des Moines. If you decide to stay, we'll open whatever accounts you may want right here."

"That should work nicely. Thank you."

"How much do you think you may need?"

Stumped, I was. In my young life...well, sort of young, I remembered signing up for that very class in college. It was titled "Fundamentals of Maintaining a Stately Home, While Searching for Treasure Buried by a Dead Ancestor Somewhere in the World, After Having Lost All the Clues to a Thief in the Night at a Cheap Motel in a Strange Little Seacoast Town...101." Unfortunately, the class was full, and I missed it. I tried not to laugh upon this reflection. He must have sensed my bewilderment.

"How about a hundred thousand," he suggested. "We can start with that anyway."

I grinned back at him. "Took the words right out of my mouth."

"I'll have Miss Dunston draw up the contract, while you are examining the contents of your safe-deposit box."

"Great."

After I gave him information on my Des Moines account and signed for a safe-deposit key, Farington escorted me to the vault, where I extracted the 12" x 18" x 6" deep steel box and entered a private viewing cubicle. Locking the door behind me, I set the heavy box on the counter. My hands shook, as I inserted the key and lifted the cover.

As I stood there, enraptured…captivated by the magnificent sight before me, I felt it grab hold of me. The icy hot fingers of greed encircled me, stoking the fires of my imagination, freeing latent primordial desires locked within the pretense of civility and humanity, while still chilling my heart and soul to render them nearly devoid of feeling. I knew then. I knew that I was capable of doing all those heinous, hideous things that men and women do to each other in pursuit of wealth and power. The trembling in my hands spread throughout the whole of my body, as the demon tightened its grip.

No no no! I would not give in. Grandfather's words ran echoing through my mind: "Promise me, boy. Swear to me on the grave of your dear, sweet mother that you'll not give in to the greed; that your soul will stay chaste; and when the time comes, you'll do right by me."

With all my might, I tore myself free from the grip of demon greed. Somewhere outside my body, I heard myself say, "I will! I will, Grandfather! I will do right by you. I swear to you, Grandfather!"

Of course, I wasn't the only one to have heard me; hence, the urgent knocking on the viewing room door. It was Farington, asking if I were all right.

"Oh, yes. I'm fine. I was just thinking out loud." Lying can be habitual.

"Very well. If you need anything else, don't hesitate."

"Thank you."

I took stock of my fortune. Lining either side of the box were stacks of what I took to be gold doubloons in shrink-wrap. The list said two hundred in all; ten stacks of twenty each. In the center was a myriad of jeweled rings, broaches, pendants, necklaces, and other precious ornaments that had once graced the finery on ladies and gentlemen of the court. Whose court? I don't think it mattered to Grandfather Hudson.

My heart froze for an instant. Barely visible beneath this pile of dreams was a cross, or so it appeared. Again, Grandfather's words came back. "There's an object, a cross. It's not with the rest. It cannot be kept. It must be returned."

Could it be? My fingers dug furiously through the objects to uncover the cross. I drew it out. To my dismay, the object I thought a cross turned out to be its evil, wicked double…a dagger. The rest of the objects had covered everything except that portion of the weapon where the blade met the bejeweled hilt. My eager, confused mind had mistaken the dagger for a cross. How ironic, I thought, that two symbols, so different in meaning, should appear so similar in shape. How often in history have we humans, in a fog of ignorance mixed the two up, using the dagger instead of the cross…or worse yet, using the dagger to advance the cross?

The quiet ringing of a ship's muted bell ended my speculations, and a soft voice came over the PA system. "Attention, patrons. The time is now four forty-five and Seacoast State Bank will be closing in fifteen minutes. Thank you and have a pleasant evening."

I glanced up at the small clock on the wall. I'm not sure why. I mean, it wasn't a bar or anything. They didn't have to start pushing people out early. There must be something in our human code that triggers an endorphin of distrust in our brains. Considering the events of the past twenty-four hours or so, I thought that probably not a bad thing.

Quickly, I rearranged the contents of my very own treasure chest, locked it in the drawer and headed back to Farington's office. As I raised my hand to knock gently on the door, from behind me it came again; yet another soft voice, this one with a sense of urgency, but still with the gentleness of a playful kitten.

"Mister Hudson, Mister Hudson."

My mind stopped, and my head turned…but my arm kept travelling on its downward arc toward what should have been the glass door. Now, I sometimes think it would have been a good idea for the Creator (whomever or whatever he, she or it may be) to have given us at least one eye in the back of our heads; or in my case, between the third and fourth knuckles of the right hand. Luckily, the door with which I should have made contact was ornate glass; and therefore, my knuckles were not travelling at a high rate of speed, as they made contact with the pliable cartilage of a human nose.

Upon reflection, I really do think we had the makings of a very good quartet.

"Oh!" came the soft trill of Miss Ainsley, the secretary who had been calling my name: mezzo soprano.

"Oh!" Me: Alto.

"Oh!" Farington. Tenor.

"Ohhhhhh!" The hapless victim provided a booming baritone.

I forced myself to turn and see what damage my inattentiveness had inflicted on another human being. The man was short, which is probably why I made contact with his nose instead of his chest. A mostly bald, thirty-five-ish pate topped a round face that was now covered by a chubby, stubby hand and fingers, as the poor man cupped his throbbing proboscis.

"Oh! Excuse me, sir! I am SO sorry!" I crawled all over myself, apologizing. "I...I didn't see you open the door and...and..."

"That's all right," he interrupted. "It's all right. Nothing broken. Just a little bump. That's all...I think." The man pulled his cupped hand away briefly and stared into it. "See. No blood." His eyes were curiously large and appeared brown in color.

Farington looked closely at the stout man's snout. Other than a slight redness, it showed no outward signs of distress. "Miss Ainsley," Farington said. "Perhaps you should get some ice put on Mister... uh..." He hesitated.

"Chamberlin," the short man offered quickly. "Walt Chamberlin...no relation to Wilt," he added with a grin, referring to one of the greatest basketball players who ever lived, seven-foot, one-inch Wilt Chamberlin.

"Oh, yes. Of course. How silly of me to forget," Farington said. The amiable Miss Ainsley's eyes narrowed in apparent confusion. Farington continued, "Well, Miss Ainsley, see that Mister Chamberlin gets some ice on that nose, please."

"Uh...yes, of course. Right away, Mister Farington. I'll have Joanne take care of it," she answered, leading the still-chuckling Chamberlin toward the employee's lounge.

When they were gone, I turned to Farington. "I'm really sorry, Mister Farington. I hope I didn't ruin any kind of business deal for you."

"Oh, no," he assured me. "He...uh, Mister Chamberlin just stopped by for a chat. Nothing serious."

I thought for a moment and then concluded it was better just to be on my way.

"Well, I was just coming to tell you that I was leaving and wanted to make sure everything was all set before I left."

"Yes, of course. Everything is set. We've contacted your bank in Iowa, and your line of credit is all arranged. You're a rich man now, Mister Hudson. Enjoy." He put a hand on my shoulder, and we began walking toward the entrance.

"Thank you, Mister Farington," I said, as we approached the door. "I do have some loose ends to tie up before I settle in to a life of leisure."

"Loose ends?" he queried. "Oh, you mean getting the house cleaned and ready."

"Ready? For what?"

"Occupancy, Mister Hudson. Occupancy."

"Oh, yes. That could be quite a job."

"I'm sure it will be," he replied. "I would be more than happy to contact a professional cleaning service to help you out. It's a hard-working, honest company. I use them myself."

"That would be fine," I replied. "Thank you. I appreciate it."

"Not a problem, Mister Hudson. We're here to help. You have a fine evening now."

With that, we said our goodbyes, shook hands, and I retired to the lovely Miss Ainsley's desk to sign papers authorizing transfer of funds to my bank back in Des Moines. It was nearly dusk when I stepped out into the fading light. As I stood there, staring into the setting sun, I thought about going directly to the library, but I wasn't sure what to look for yet. Without the diary, my information was limited to the little bit I'd been able to read in it, and the numbers Grandfather Hudson had driven into my head. Not much. I searched my circuits for anything else. Let's see. There was the cross and the church some distance east of Lima, Peru. I thought until my head began to hurt. As I got into my Volkswagen, I glanced over my shoulder to check for traffic. My eye caught a sign in the window of a shop across the street. "Portrait Studio." Portrait? That's it! Grandfather's words were, "Within its frame, ye'll find the way." Hmmm. I had just enough time before dark to make a return visit to Hudson house and locate the portrait. I should collect as much information as possible before I go scouring the library.

I really didn't hate school as a youngster. I did, however, have my share of made-up maladies manufactured to purposely prohibit my attendance at that fine institution of lower learning, Emerson Elementary School. I never was too sure if it had been named in honor of a poet or a radio. In any case, when I finally did realize that my mischievous malaise was no longer sustainable and I had no choice but to rejoin the world of the healthy, I…would…panic. What did I miss? How much homework would I have to catch up? *Tons* of it. Oh no! Now I just can't go back! Run away. That's it. Run away and join the circus. No. Can't do that. I'm afraid of animals. What to do? Fear would worm its way into my churning stomach, and I really would make myself ill. I didn't want to go back there, but I knew I had to. With each step that brought me closer to Emerson Elementary, my angst exponentially increased to a point approaching terror.

It was then I would reach down deep and bring up one of dear old dad's philosophical gems. "Nothing's ever as bad as you think, son. Fear only makes it seem that way." But then, dear old dad never had to endure Miss Daumsauger's tirades either. Nor had he ever discovered a dead body in his attic.

My mind, my heart, my spirit, and my churning stomach all regressed back to those disquieting days of Emerson Elementary angst, as I turn my car into the Hudson house driveway once again and an uncertain, even tenuous future. I felt good at having the courage to go back to a house in which I was sure there had been a murder; a house that now seemed to own me more than I did it. This, I was doing in spite of my grave misgivings. Had I known this was only one of the tribulations I would ultimately endure, I would have.... Well, I'm not sure what I would have done. Perhaps sometimes it's better, after all, that we don't know what awaits us on the other side of the mountain or the river or the door...or life.

Reaching deep and grabbing another handful of Daddy's courage, I parked the car, entered the gate and walked boldly up to the front door, key in hand. I stopped. This time, I decided to try the door first to see if it were locked...and it was indeed locked. Feeling quite cocky, I turned the key with all the authority of a jailer (with whom I'd had all the experience I ever wanted...and will ever want) and strode fearlessly through the open door.

Now, when one strides fearlessly somewhere, one often is too confident and proud of one's ability to do so to watch where one is going. I found the consequence of this arrogance staring me nose to nose on the floor of the entrance hallway, its massive jaws dripping saliva from the razor-sharp canines that were about to rip my skinny little throat to shreds.

"AAAGGGHHH!" My ear-splitting shriek could, I was sure, be heard by the sheriff on duty...in the next county. My fear-wracked body bounced back off the floor as if I were on a trampoline. *Wham!* My back hit the wall, followed closely by my head.

"OWWWW!" My hand flew to the back of my head...as if that would stop the pain. If nothing else, the throbbing there took my hysterical mind off the imaginary predator that now mocked me from its place on the floor. In my defense, I must say that portrait of the huge gray wolf about to close on its prey was so realistically and beautifully painted that anyone might have thought it real. True or false, that thought soothed my injured pride, if not my injured head. The painting's glass and frame were shattered, shards and splinters strewn everywhere. Near it lay the overturned telephone stand (sans device) that had jumped out and bitten my right ankle, causing my encounter on the floor with the big bad wolf.

With my mind's eye and my real eyes again operating on the same frequency, I looked around. Other pictures lay shattered on the floor. I cautiously ventured farther into the house. Table and desk drawers were open, their contents flung about the room. Books were yanked off their shelves, opened and cast aside. In short, the place had been ransacked.

Why? Why must I step into a quagmire of mystery every time I cross the threshold in my own house? Why? Why? All the paintings and photographs had been ripped down from the walls and tossed aside. Obviously, the perpetrators had been searching for a wall safe. Then it hit me. Grandfather's portrait! Quickly, I picked my way through this trash bin, toward the door of Grandfather's office. It was open, its contents suffering the same fate as the other violated rooms.

There on the floor, behind the beautiful dark oak desk, lay the tattered, shattered likeness of Great-Great-Great-Grandfather James Bartholomew Hudson the First. The canvass had been ripped off its frame and the frame sides separated. Picking my way through the debris, I knelt down to recover Grandfather's portrait and turned it over. My heart froze, and my blood turned to ice. There, staring me in the face, was the self-same James Bartholomew Hudson the First that had haunted my dream. The face was identical, right down to the well-trimmed beard. I hadn't entered this room at all on the previous night. There's no way I could have known what Grandfather really looked like unless…unless…

"Freeze! Put your hands behind your head, stand up and turn around…slowly!"

The voice sounded familiar, and I was getting used to following those commands. Doing as he said, I turned. There are some experiences that just cannot adequately be explained to another human being. Among them would be the thrill of love, the pain of giving birth, the exhilaration of reaching the summit on Everest, and…oh yes, the paralyzing fear when staring down the barrel of a nine-millimeter Glock that is pointed straight at your heart. Luckily for me, the man holding it was none other than my new old friend, Sergeant Scarecrow. He must have seen the absolute fear on my face. His demeanor relaxed, and he holstered his gun.

Oh, Mister Hudson," he began. "I thought it might be you, but I wasn't sure. Didn't mean to frighten you, but we do have to take every precaution."

"I quite understand, Officer. Not a problem." I hesitated. "But...how did you...I mean, I didn't call you."

"One of your neighbors did," he explained. "She heard a blood-curdling scream and became concerned."

"No doubt," I said. "This came as quite a shock when I walked through the door." I wasn't about to tell him I had been frightened senseless by a painting.

"Uh..." He acted like he really didn't want to ask his next question. "Uh...have you noticed anything missing?" The look on my face was enough. "I know. I know," he added quickly, "but it's something we're required to ask. I'll just put down that you haven't been able to determine that yet."

I chuckled and nodded. "That could take until the next millennium."

"Was the door locked?"

"Yes. Yes, it was."

"What about the back door?"

I wanted to ask him, what back door? That's how little I knew about the place yet, but I didn't get the chance.

"Forced." The answer came from somewhere behind Sergeant Scarecrow. Presently, its originating officer appeared at the door. His being a rookie, or nearly so, was painfully obvious. He was wearing no chevrons or longevity pins, and he was wearing a tie, something that would make a perfect choking instrument during a tussle with a belligerent drunk. Besides, he looked as if he had just cut twelfth grade chemistry class to tag along with his big brother, Scarecrow.

"Well," offered Scarecrow, "I'm sure Lieutenant Trevor will have the crime unit come in and dust for prints. Not that it will do a lot of good."

"What should I do about the back?" The words stumbled out before I realized that Sergeant Scarecrow was not responsible for repairing my back door. But being the affable man he was, he offered a solution.

"I got a brother-in-law that's a contractor. I think I can get him over here to get it fixed yet tonight. He owes me anyway."

"I'd appreciate that very much," I said. "Just have him send the bill to Mister Farington over at the bank. I'll give him a heads up."

"Sure thing. I'll call my sister as soon as we're done here."

"Great. Thank you again."

"Have you checked the rest of the house?" he asked.

"No. I haven't had the chance yet. I wanted to check on Grandfather Hudson's portrait first. It's an heirloom now, I guess. As far as I know, it's the only likeness we have of him."

Scarecrow stared at the broken frame and canvass. "Too bad," he said, shaking his head. "Never ceases to amaze me why some people just have to destroy things." He hesitated. "I mean, stealing is one thing, but this...this..." He gave a big sigh. "This makes no sense at all."

"Some people just have to steal from somebody, I guess. If they weren't burglars, they'd probable be corporate CEOs or politicians," I answered.

"Or pirates," he quipped.

I chuckled and nodded at that one, but in reality, he was right. For all their fame, their folklore, their historical majesty, pirates were after all, just plain crooks. They stole other people's property for themselves...and often killed innocent people in the process. There can be no honor in that.

"Tell you what," Scarecrow offered. "I'll have Officer Wojohowski accompany you through the rest of the house, and I'll try to get hold of my brother-in-law."

Wojohowski, huh? Looked more like Bambi to me. That's what I resolved to call him...not out loud, of course. Out loud I said, "Fine."

While the good Scarecrow went out to make his calls, Officer Bambi and I explored the rest of the house, the condition of which seemed to mimic that of the downstairs rooms. Suddenly, I thought of the chest. The chest! Of course. Why hadn't I thought of that before?

Up the steep stairs I flew past Mr. Ugly and straight to that same heavy oaken chest that had once held my dreams, my future...my life. It was there, closed. Now, by the light filtering through the small oval attic windows, I could see with unnerving clarity the details of my previous visit.

The chest was as impressive as I remembered it to be. Thick oak boards held together by black metal bands made it a respectable-looking treasure chest...enough to sate the fantasies of dreamers everywhere. However, this was no dream. This quest, begun as a boyish adventure in Des Moines, had all the potential to become a menacing nightmare.

In the dust-filtered light, I could see streaks and blobs of red paint that had run around the left side and under the chest to pool in the hollows of the uneven floor boards. Having seen this attic...this treasure trove of antiquities, only in the narrow glare of a flashlight, I was awestruck at the sheer volume of objects relegated to this ancestral purgatory...neither utilized nor discarded.

Here and there, I could see evidence of human intrusion into the world of unwanted doodads and thingamajigs. Dust was absent where things had been moved around. Footprints led to various corners of the large attic, whether made by the intruders, the police or...oh, dear...the killer. That thought chilled my bones. I timidly peeked over the treasure chest to reassure myself that the body I knew was behind it was indeed made of something other than flesh and bones. Yup, there it was, naked as a jay bird and the perfect model for death. The mannequin's eyes looked to have not the distant, detached stare of a runway model, but the mournful pleading of a hapless soul about to meet his demise. I wondered if the real victim had looked that way just before...before...

*BAM!* Down, heart, down! Get out of my throat! The sound of Sergeant Scarecrow's feet pounding up the attic steps mercifully pulled my morose mind back from the brink. He stopped at the top and looked around.

"Where's Wojohowski?" he asked.

"Not a clue," I answered.

"Well, he was supposed to stay with you to make a list of missing items."

"I hardly think that would be possible at this point."

"Procedures, Mister Hudson. He's a rookie. Got to get used to procedures." He took a few more steps into the attic and shifted gears. "Anyway, I got hold of my brother-in-law. He's on his way over now. If you're done up here, we could go meet him outside."

"All right," I agreed. I steered clear of any reference to my previous visit in this home of horror.

I turned to leave, then stopped and looked back at the tracks in the dust that led to a corner behind some characteristically rustic oak barrels. I wondered if they were filled with rum. I decided I'd have to check that out someday, but not today. The tracks I reasoned had probably been made by the killer. I shuddered again. Why did I even want to own, let alone live in, a house that always makes me shudder? Humans are funny creatures.

Turning back, I stopped suddenly again, nearly causing a rear-end collision from Sergeant Scarecrow. I stared for a long time at that beautiful, ugly, warm-hearted, stone-cold creature that had saved my life and remembered the solemn vow I'd made. Then, with Scarecrow staring incredulously at this pragmatic, possessed midwestern wacko, I puckered up and planted that big, fat, wet sloppy kiss right smack-dab on that gargoyle's lips...telling myself that it was indeed a girl gargoyle, although my gratitude was such that it really wouldn't have made a difference. Coming up for air, I grinned at the wide-eyed Scarecrow.

"Hey, man," he said, throwing his hands up in front of himself. "Whatever tops your ice cream, you know? I didn't see a thing. Who am I to judge?"

With that, I broke into a raucous laughter; something I hadn't done since my encounter with the Frankenstein Monster, et al. I couldn't count the maniacal whoops from my first visit here, since that was from a fear-induced safety valve, not the mirthful musings I felt now.

We both giggled and chuckled our way down the steps and out into the front yard, where Scarecrow's brother-in-law was waiting for his assignment. Those business negotiations being somewhat mundane and the contractor, whose name was Boris or Morris or something like that, agreeing to button the place up "tighter than two elephants in a Volkswagen," then drop off all the keys to me at the motel. Scarecrow said he'd see that the patrols would go by about every hour or so, just to help deter any lingering thoughts the perps may have about returning.

With that settled, I returned to the house to retrieve Grandfather Hudson's portrait. In Grandfather's...er, my study, I began rolling up the painting, taking care to brush off any glass fragments, and tucked it under my arm. I stared at the unusually decorated carved oak frame, which was not splintered, but still in pieces. I decided to gather them up also. Good move. Then, thanking Scarecrow, Bambi, and contractor Boris Morris again, I climbed into my VW Bug (after first checking for elephants) and drove wearily back to my very humble abode at the Poop Deck Motel.

Dear old mom often said that tension tires the body out faster and more completely than does a good workout. Of that, I was marginally living proof. A candy bar and a soda were quite sufficient for my evening meal, and I simply collapsed onto my somewhat lumpy bed, fully expecting to be once again drawn into the world of the undead and encounter one James Bartholomew Hudson the First. However, much to my surprise and my body's delight, no such journey happened; and my superb imitation of a log actually lasted all night long.

# CHAPTER SIX

They say (whomever "they" are) that after a wild night of revelry and drink, one's senses are debilitated to an extreme. I sort of wished that had been the case, so at least I could have had some fun and good reason for waking up with my mind shrouded in fog and its horn blasting between my ears. Forcing my arm out from underneath my dead-weight body, I slapped for the alarm buzzer on the clock. The foghorn stopped, but the fog didn't clear. I raised my head and, for a moment, wondered where I was. Spotting Grandfather's rolled up portrait, surrounded by disjointed pieces of its frame, lying on the same accursed coffee table from which my life had been snatched the night I arrived.

After completing my morning duties, I rolled Grandfather's portrait out on the table. It was indeed the same distinguished-looking cutthroat I'd encountered in my dream...if it was a dream. He was wearing a blue double-breasted blazer with shiny gold buttons and gold braids about the cuffs. The artist had captured his features very well, at least when compared to the James Bartholomew Hudson the First that I had met.

My eyes began to methodically scan every square inch of the painting for any sign of a clue to the whereabouts of Grandfather's treasure. Perhaps a map in the background hidden in a picture, maybe. Nope. Nothing like that. The hair, the beard, the face...still nothing. Hey! What about the brush strokes? Any detectable pattern? Nope.

For nearly an hour, I checked, rechecked, scratched my head and uttered unmentionables under my breath. Exhausted and nearly out of expletives, I decided to try again later with a fresh mind…if I still had one left by that time. My eye caught one of the buttons on Grandfather's blazer again. It appeared to have a number pattern on it. I looked more closely. Definitely the number 5. There were two vertical rows of three buttons each. I stared at the next button down. Yes. There was another 5! The last one down on that side was a 3. On the other side, the top button showed an 8; the one down, a 7; and the bottom, a 6. Finding a pen, I wrote them down on a sheet of the stationery from the nightstand.

"Five, five, three," I muttered to myself. "Eight, seven, six."

They sounded awfully familiar.

"Five, five, three; Eight, seven, six," I said out loud again.

Yes. Of course. My mind's eye peeked through the narrow windows into the holding cells of each number Grandfather had given to me. Let's see, 5. Yup. That's there. Another 5. OK. Now, a 3. Yes. And an 8, a 7, and finally a 6, which looked a little worse for the wear, after our wrestling match. Wow. All accounted for.

So, it seems Grandfather didn't completely trust his descendants' intellect (or perhaps he was just cautious), so he built in a back-up plan. Hmmm. I wondered what else he had doubled up on. I decided to ponder that a while. Picking up the pieces of the frame, I laid them carefully on top of the portrait, placing them side by side. The beautifully varnished dark oak had the most interesting raised patterns of contours and swirls, occasionally extending clear out to the edge of the board on one or both sides.

Arranging them neatly, I thought how curious it was that two of the raised patterns, when butted side by side, were perfectly matched…as did two more farther on down the board. Having toiled over my share of picture puzzles as a youngster, this piqued my curiosity. Taking the next board, I tried it various ways and on both sides of the ones already matched. By turning it end for end, it matched perfectly with one of them. The last one was easy to figure out, fitting right in between what was the second and third boards. I stepped back.

The first thing that caught my eye was the steepness of the patterns. It looked almost like a relief map of…of…maybe an island?

Duh. Color me stupid. Yes. How could I be so blind? It was a relief map of an island. Looking more closely, I saw what must be two small coves, one on either side of the steep walnut-shaped dome that was my very own treasure island. But which one?

The buttons. The buttons that contained the shape of each number Grandfather had made me memorize. Map coordinates, of course! Taking another sheet of stationery from the nightstand, I made a rough sketch of the island and put both papers in my pocket. Forgetting all about the rumbling of my empty stomach, I headed out the door and straight to the library.

The library was one of Mr. Carnegie's gifts to a nation thirsting for knowledge. The stately brownstone stood erect, like a stern headmaster keeping a watchful eye on its adolescent neighbors, the ice-cream parlor and the music store. At the bottom of the massive steeps, I surveyed the Roman columns, holding up a short portico. The brushed aluminum doors and windows looked out of place amid the ornate stone structure (added, I was sure, by some well-meaning but aesthetically challenged administrator). Well, I guess it did keep the old building warmer in the winter and cooler in the summer; but couldn't they at least have painted them?

Nevertheless, it was an impressive building built by an impressive man in an impressive era. The gilded age of the nineteenth century was gilded, indeed, for those barons of industry that forged empires on the backs of their workers who often toiled long hours in dangerous jobs for little pay. For them, the age was not so gilded. I often wondered if the philanthropic endeavors of these captains of industry were attempts to mask their individual serfdoms from the general populace, or perhaps to color their own legacies in the eyes of history with rose-tinted glasses. Whatever their motives, it cannot be denied that their gifts were of enormous value to a growing nation.

I pulled hard on the cold metal handle and passed through into the lobby. To the right of the dark oak horseshoe-shaped main desk, open double doors led to a nineteenth century reading room, full of heavy oak tables and straight-backed wooden chairs. On the left, stacks of books containing the treasures of the ages…including mine.

Stepping up to the exquisitely carved desk, I was greeted by a matronly woman who was wearing atop her head what looked to be a hairy hamburger bun pierced by a shish kabob skewer.

"Well, hello, Mister Hudson," she gushed. "It is such an honor to meet you."

"Thank you," I answered, somewhat taken aback by her recognition of me. Did EVERYBODY in this backwater burg know me on sight? "The pleasure is all mine," I continued. "You have such a lovely town, full of such gracious people, that I dare say I might never leave."

"We're counting on it," she replied, flashing a sort of Mona Lisa smile at me. Hmmm. I wondered how I should take that?

"Well," I said, "I'd like to do some research while I'm here."

"Pirates, eh?"

"Among other things, yes."

She continued, "You're going to find a fine collection of nautical history in the second-floor stacks to my right, and of course, you can see the reference section on the other side." She gestured to her left.

"Thank you, Miss…uh…"

"Parsons. Audrey Parsons. I'm the head librarian here."

"Well, Miss Parsons, I may need to check out a few items, but I haven't as yet applied for a library card. Will that be a problem?"

She grinned and reached into a drawer. "Kind of anticipated that, Mister Hudson," she said, pulling out a small plastic card with my name on it and sliding it across the desk. "Not a problem." This latest surprise warranted some explanations.

"Miss Parsons," I began, "it seems as if everybody in town knows who I am, why I'm here and even what I look like." She looked around quickly, as if to see who might be listening.

"The town has been anticipating this day for a long time."

"But why?" I asked. "What stake does an entire town have in my finding my great-great-great-grandfather's treasure…if there even is one?" I paused. "And why tear my house apart?"

This seemed to puzzle her. "Huh?" Her face took on a genuinely curious look. "I'm afraid I don't know anything about that, Mister Hudson." She paused again. "You say, somebody ransacked that beautiful old house of yours? Why…why, that's just…just… criminal!"

"Yes. That's what the police thought," I answered with just a hint of sarcasm.

Her eyes narrowed slightly, as she spoke. "And you have no idea who…" She stopped abruptly, as a dumpy middle-aged man in a rumpled brown suit slowly shuffled by. Her eyes followed his progress past the desk. "…who might have done it?"

"Madam," I continued with polite incredulity. "I have been in your fair city for a total of three days. For all I know, it could have been you."

"Oh no," she startled. "That wasn't my…uh, I didn't mean you personally. I meant the police. They might have an idea who could be involved."

She had stumbled. Words she hadn't meant to say raced out her lips before she could stop them. I wondered, why? What might she have said? I pondered this just an instant, then dismissed it as a wandering mind…maybe.

"Yes. Well, I guess that is what the police are paid to do, isn't it?"

"Yes. Yes, it is." She paused. "So, Mister Hudson, I imagine you're anxious to get started on your quest."

"Well, Miss Parsons, I'm not sure 'quest' is the right word. I'd prefer to think that I'm just a guy trying to learn as much about his roots as he can."

"Indeed," she said with finality. "Then, let's get you started." She came around the desk, took my arm and led me to a small private reading room that appeared to be about five by six feet with a lone table, chair, and a reading lamp with a green shade. "You'll be able to concentrate better here," she said, opening the door.

"This will be just fine," I answered.

She continued. "The card catalogue is over there, next to the wall on the left, and periodicals are in the room just beyond that stairwell going to the second-floor stacks." She pointed toward a small circular stairway that curled its way skyward to a large steel deck, packed with the wisdom of the world. "If you need anything else, just whistle," she said, turning back toward her desk. She stopped and looked back with a grin. "Figuratively speaking, of course."

"Of course," I agreed, as she continued back to her desk.

For the next several hours, I plowed through the countless volumes of facts, figures, names and dates that made up local history here in this little seacoast village. I learned Grandfather Hudson seemed to materialize out of thin air about 1880…already wealthy. Considering the encounter I'd had with Grandfather, I mused that it seemed to be typical of him. Nobody could track down his origin. I wondered what they'd say, if I told them where he was now, and how I knew it. I concluded they'd probably have a chuckle about it…as they were locking the door to my padded cell.

Piracy as a major scourge had all but disappeared by that time, and rumors of buried treasure ran rampant throughout the country…nay, the world. Despite modern technology, it's still a big world and tracking down which hoard may have been Grandfather's seemed daunting. I decided to start with what I knew.

One, Grandfather was a pirate. He stole other people's possessions on the high seas at gunpoint.

Two, one of his victims was apparently in or from Lima, Peru.

Three, it possibly had something to do with a church. He made me promise to return a cross to a church East of Lima.

Now given the times, how many churches might there have been in the vicinity of Lima, Peru? For hours, I paged through books and magazine articles on pirates, plunder, and Peru. Most of these were unlikely prospects because of the timeframe or because the plunder had been either recovered or sunk at sea. Getting somewhat disheartened, I opened an old book near the bottom of my possibilities file.

In the interest of expediency, I scanned the index at the back for any mention of Peru. There was one, but having chased several false leads already dampened any exhilaration. I turned to a chapter on Cocos Island and began reading. The more I read, the drier became the wet towel of reality that sometimes covers our dreams when our hearts become heavy with discouragement. By the end of that chapter, I felt that I'd really stumbled upon a likely possibility. I began drawing parallels to what I knew and speculated about Grandfather Hudson's life.

Grandfather died in 1902 at the ripe old age of ninety-seven… at least, that's what the obituary I found for him confirmed. He had no birth certificate that could be found. He and Great-Great-Great-Grandmother Marion had two children: James Bartholomew Junior and Althea, a girl. James Junior apparently was an early bloomer. He began his sailing career on a coastal fishing vessel at an early age, married at an early age and died in a shipwreck at an early age… childless. That meant the bloodline from Grandfather had to be passed down through Althea Hudson…who naturally would have married and assumed her husband's name; and that in all probability would not have been Hudson. That's undoubtedly why it took so long to produce another James Bartholomew Hudson. The trust company had to wait until a female descendant, which would have been my mother, married an unrelated Hudson and named her son James Bartholomew.

The various accounts of the treasure from Lima that was supposedly hidden on Cocos varied somewhat from book to book, but taking a composite picture of the incident puts the timeframe anywhere from 1820 to about 1823, and that would put Grandfather Hudson about in his mid to late teens. That a young man of such an age would turn to piracy is not beyond the realm of possibility, especially given the time and uncertainty of his actual birth date. I decided this possibility had the most promise.

Now that I had possible beginning and end points (those being Lima, Peru and an island located somewhere in the Pacific Ocean), to the maps I flew. Fast and thorough are two diametrically opposed terms. The point at which they do converge is usually named luck. I happened to be standing at that point in my search when my finger crossed over a tiny island on the map, some three hundred miles off the coast of Costa Rica.

"Cocos," I muttered to myself, as my finger drew an imaginary circle around it. Quickly, I sought out the nearest latitude line. "Five degrees and about…fifty-three minutes north," I continued. Now, to the longitude. "Eighty-seven degrees and about…six minutes, west."

I'm sure my excited mind honed in on those particular precise minutes because that's what I wanted them to be, but no matter. There were no other islands even close that could be mistaken for *my* treasure island. A minute or two off one way or the other would not have changed things.

My hands trembled at the very thought, but I had to make sure...dead sure. As I stared at the tiny green speck in the light blue sea, my mind folded into self. Like a jailer on his rounds, I strode the corridors of my mind, searching for the cells in which I sequestered the page numbers Grandfather Hudson had sworn me to safeguard. The tap tap tap of my hobnailed boots echoed loudly through the cellblocks of my memories. My keys jangled a rhythmic dirge, as I ambled past my childhood, shrouded now in cobwebs and muddy memories. As I passed some of their cells, I couldn't help glancing in to see how these little slices of my life—the essence of who I had become—had fared, since their incarceration in my brain. Scientists say that every thought, every emotion, every sensory experience we have ever had is locked somewhere in this marvelous mechanism of incalculable capacity we call a brain.

There were Christmases in winter and picnics on Saylorville Lake in summer that would occasionally present themselves to me. Their laughter, smells, and sights were like catnip to a tabby, and a smile would form across my face in spite of the seriousness of my current quest. Peeking through the door slot of one, I watched myself trying in vain to swim like many of the other kids, but the signals between my brain and body were apparently shorted out by the water, and I would ultimately perform a wonderful imitation of a rock.

Not all of the memories were fun, however, or even pleasant. Those I sped quickly past, not daring to glance into their lonely cells and relive the pain. A natural defense mechanism, I suppose. Well... except for one. That composite cell, that hidden part of our head and our heart in which abide the love we have found and lost...all put together in a mixture of joy so powerful it hurts and sorrow so strong it numbs the whole being.

She stood there. Through the murky mist of a million tears, I gazed upon that smile; the beautiful, disarming, dastardly, deceitful, delightful, delectable smile that captured the soul before cleaving the heart in two. For that eternal instant I stood there, devoid of any armor, defenseless against her onslaught of perplexing passion and laborless love. As she glided smoothly toward me, I inhaled one last time the essence of her dangerous beauty; then, I wrenched myself clear of her fatal grip as if a voltage had held me fast, and I had only one shot at escaping with my life.

Picking myself up from the cold stone cellblock floor, I looked back for just a moment at the cell wherein was kept both my most unbelievable love and unbearable pain.

"Wow," I told myself with delusory resolve. "I've *got* to stop doing that. Just got to."

I continued my way past various stages of me until I reached cell block 28-F. Let's see, cells 2845 through 2850. Yup. There they are. I peeked in at the first 5. There it sat, rocking back and forth on its rounded base and looking so forlorn. For about half a heartbeat, I felt sorry for the poor creature. Then, a streak of greed reminded me of my mission. Check. I proceeded to 53. A five and a three. OK. Next, 87. Eight and seven. Check. The last one, I was a little nervous about. I had no way of knowing whether it had been injured in our little scuffle the other night. But I knew I had to make sure.

A little apprehensive, I peeked in. He must have heard me coming. I'd always heard that sixes were intuitive, independent little cusses. I guess I should not have been surprised to see hard, cold eyes staring back at me through slits that reminded me of gunports on a rampart. If looks could kill… I slinked quietly away toward the exit.

Once my mind returned to the task at hand, the corners of my mouth lightly touched the tips of my earlobes in a consuming smile that would do any Cheshire cat proud. The grid coordinates converged right on the island that legend says harbors one of the world's most fabulous treasures. Quickly, I checked some of my notes. It's reported to contain gold, silver chalices, two life-sized gold statues of the Virgin Mary, and of course, a number of jewel-encrusted crucifixes. I wondered, which one was Grandfather's?

Pulling out the rough sketch I'd made of the island pictured on Grandfather's portrait frame, I compared it to the island on the map.

Proportions were a little off, but the two bays and rocky coast were unmistakable.

"Wow," I breathed quietly, as I plopped in a stupor onto the hard oak chair. My eyes saw beyond the dull blue wall in front of me. I had that thousand-yard stare in a ten-foot room, as one of my veteran friends called it. For a time, just one of those fleeting lifetimes when the real world disappears into the fog of boyhood fancy, I was there, on my very own treasure island, hacking through dense jungle and fighting pirates to find one of the world's most fabulous treasures.

# CHAPTER SEVEN

The remainder of that day, I spent gathering as much information as I could, not only on Cocos Island, but the history of Lima, Peru from 1800 to the present. To say that this packed a whole peck of papers in a one-pound pouch would be a mouthful...so, I won't. Suffice it to say that my next excursion back to the world of here and now wasn't until the softest voice yet in this city of gentle sounds warned me that the library was about to close with me in it. I looked up at the speaker on the wall in front of me, the one with the blue-tinted globe hanging below it. Funny, I thought, how humans will stare at the source of a sound even when it's from an inanimate object, as if it were staring back at us.

I checked my cheap electric Timex. Almost 8:00 PM. Quickly, I stuffed my pile of notes, photocopied maps, timelines, and doodles into an oversized manila envelope, shut off the light and headed for the front door.

"Find what you needed?" asked a familiar female voice from behind me. I turned to see Miss Parsons approaching from her desk.

"Not sure, "I said, "but I must compliment you on the quality of your information here. I really found it quite thorough."

"Thank you," she replied. "We've been very diligent in selecting our stack material. We have an extensive collection of piracy legends." Her eyes either twinkled with pride or glowed with foreboding mischief. Hard to tell which.

"Yes, indeed," I answered. She simply stood there, smiling for an awkward instant. "Well, have a pleasant evening, Miss Parsons," I continued, as I pushed through the heavy double doors.

Her reply was drowned out by the clock imbedded at the peak of the massive roof sounding out its song: *ding-ding, ding-ding.* Four bells. That's 10:00 PM on the first watch. I thought of the great actress, Bette Davis, ascending stairs in the 1950 classic, *All About Eve*, as I descended the stone steps to my car. "Fasten your seat belts." I chuckled to myself. "It's going to be a bumpy night."

As it turned out, the only thing bumpy that night was the cheap mattress on my cheap bed in my cheap motel room. Nor did Grandfather decide to grace me with his presence…or past, as the case might be. Before retiring for only my second full night's sleep since arriving here, I sorted through my treasure trove of information. The deeper I got, the more I realized just what a daunting task I had. I decided to make a list of what I needed to even get started:

1. If I were going to Peru and Costa Rica, I'd need a passport and visas. That will take some time to arrange.

2. Shots. Yuk!

3. Transportation. I thought it not likely the island would have an airport or even a helipad. That left only travelling some three hundred miles in a boat. Wow! Did I look forward to that…not.

4. Equipment. But what kind? Picks? Shovels? Dynamite? Not a clue.

Help. I needed help. There I was with the key to finding a one-hundred-million-dollar treasure in the middle of an ocean on an island infested with…God only knows what, and not a clue on how to begin. Yes, I needed help; but who could I trust? I was the proverbial stranger in a very strange land. I thought perhaps I should return to Iowa and try to enlist the aid of some adventurous friends. That would be the most logical step. But first, I needed to get Grandfather's diary back. That was my focus, as I settled into bed and closed my baby blues; uh, one baby blue eye and one…what? Ghastly green eye? I chuckled, as I slowly drifted into another dreamless sleep. It's always good to go to sleep smiling. We don't do enough of that either.

Saturday morning gave no indication that I was about to embark, willingly or otherwise, on the kind of adventure that young kids dream to have and old kids lament they didn't. After a hearty motel continental breakfast (he says, facetiously) of doughnuts and coffee that would curl one's eyebrows, I was off to my new home on Buford Drive.

Much to my surprise, the cleaning crew had done an absolutely marvelous job of turning the trash bin that had been left by my intruders into a respectable-looking domicile once again. Even the glass had been replaced in the portrait frames. My gaze shifted to the ravenous jaws of my lupine tormentor, locked harmlessly now in a new oaken cage, hung on the wall some seven feet above the spot where he had tried to rip out my throat. A small smirk crept upon my face.

"Not so tough now, are you?" I taunted. I'm sure it was just the willies brought on by four days of stress, but I could swear that animal snarled at my insolence.

Moving quickly on, I finally had a chance to make more than a cursory examination of the stately home Grandfather had built. Not only had the cleaning crew thoroughly cleaned up the ransacking mess, but they had dusted the entire house and even replaced or cleaned the dustcovers on the furniture. Lifting the cover off one easy chair in the parlor, I contemplated its workmanship, which was exquisite.

The fabric was a mild blue, sea-green and brown pattern of sky, sea, palm trees, and sand. How appropriate, I mused. The longer I stared at the pattern, the more familiar it looked. Starting somewhere on my left-hand side of the overstuffed back was a D-shaped blue area. Rising from there to my right were rocks, cliffs, and a dense jungle. How odd. The pattern was certainly not symmetrical at all, as I had expected. Just to the left side of the chair stood a love seat with what seemed to be an unusually high back; and to its left, what I assumed was the twin to the chair I was currently examining. Hmmmm.

Taking the dustcover off the first chair, I stood and contemplated it from a few feet away. I could see certainly what looked like the coastline of a small bay on the left and mountainous hills on the right. That would be Chatham Bay. My eyes shifted to the other chair. Could it be? Stepping closer, I whisked off the cover. My heart began to patter like a school boy getting his first kiss. The general pattern was nearly a mirror image of the first chair…nearly, but not exactly. And that is what intrigued me. Had these fabrics been made in a factory, they would almost certainly be exact mirror images of each other, simply as a cost-saving measure. No, I thought more likely they were handwoven.

Pushing the second chair beside the opposite end of the love seat, I stepped back again. The unmistakable shape of an island with which I was becoming all too familiar stretched from one chair back across the camel-backed love seat and onto the opposite chair. A wide grin made its way across my serious face. Good ol' Grandfather had built in yet another backup plan. This was more proof to me how desperate he was to ensure his saving grace—that would be me—would find the jewel-bedecked cross that would finally set his soul free. That means he must have already known what his fate would be when his earthly journey was complete.

I pondered this a moment. A wave of sadness and empathy washed across me. The words of Shakespeare's *Hamlet* echoed through my mind: "…but that the dread of something after death, the undiscovered country from whose bourn no traveler returns, puzzles the will and makes us rather bear those ills we have, than fly to others we know not of."

Death is frightening enough when we know not what awaits us. But what if we do know or are convinced we do, and it's not pleasant? Grandfather must have been indeed a tortured soul toward the end of his remarkable, tragic life. This realization strengthened my resolve to honor my pledge to Grandfather and help free his soul from whatever purgatory to which it may have been sentenced. My mind raced over the maps I had copied at the library. I reasoned the bay on the left love seat back to be Weston Bay; small, mostly rocky, and with high cliffs on either side. The bay on the right love seat back was probably Wafer Bay, the most approachable landing. The chair on the right would be the highest point on the island, Mount Yglesias. A thin blue line running down from the right-hand chair at a steep angle caught my eye. A river? More accurately, the waterfall of a river. I then checked the rest of the tapestry but could find no more waterfalls. Hmmmm. I remembered from my research that Cocos

Island was replete with waterfalls of all sizes, and yet Grandfather chose to show only one. Why? Carefully, I drew a mental sketch of the waterfall's location and path, filing it away in the same cell block as the page numbers Grandfather had given me. Seeing nothing more of unusual markings on the furniture, I returned to my original intent; that of more thoroughly exploring my beautiful new home.

I was sure Norman Rockwell had used the kitchen as a backdrop for one of his paintings. The beautifully polished oak flooring, cabinets, and center worktable were magnificently crafted. The white porcelain gas stove stood on four ornately curved legs next to a white marble counter. I noticed, too, a lack of dust. The cleaning crew had not only repaired or replaced everything, they dusted too. I was impressed. But as I gazed in wonder at this den of culinary delights, there was something else missing.

Mentally, I began preparing a meal. First, I take the meat out of the antique Kelvinator refrigerator along with some milk, cheese, and a few other odds and ends. Oh, wait. The meat is not frozen. Freezer compartments were not standard in these new-fangled refrigeration units yet. Oh well. That's all right. I only bought the meat a couple of days ago. Should be still good. Well, that's one thing missing…a freezer. What else? Well, I don't have time to peel, boil, and mash potatoes, so I can just pop a couple into the microwave. Hmmm. I guess that's out too. But cleanup should be a snap. Fill the dishwasher…. Oops. Guess that's out too. I began to think that, just maybe, the good old days weren't all that good. How spoiled we have become, I thought. Then I began a slight chuckle at the thought that Grandfather Hudson had probably stood in this very same spot, lamenting over how soft we had become, since the advent of gas cookstoves and indoor privies. Indeed, Sonny and Cher, the beat goes on.

The glass in the cupboard doors were adorned with hand-painted sailing ships and other nautical themes. I wondered if Grandfather had yet another backup plan hidden in the small paintings. I carefully inspected each one but could find nothing unusual; that is, until I came upon one particular schooner (or what I imagined to be a schooner). It had a name painted on it. Despite squinting and all but placing my eyeball on the glass, I couldn't quite make out the name. Stumped for just an instant, I remembered a trick my mother had taught me what seemed now to be a century ago. Searching the cupboards, I found a clean, thick drinking glass. Putting it right up to the ships name, I twisted and turned it until the glass acted like a makeshift magnifying glass. I could just barely make out the letters: "M-A-R-Y." My face began to flush, and I had to steady the hand holding the glass with my other one. "D-E-A-R-E."

"Mary Dear," my trembling voice murmured. "Oh...my... god." The *Mary Dear*, or "Deare" as it had sometimes been written, was the ship that carried away the fabulous treasure of Lima, I'd read about at the library. My hands shook, as I put the glass back into the cupboard. The next panel over on the cupboard was an island with a very familiar shape. Cocos Island was unmistakable, and the *Mary Deare* was headed right for it. Grandfather was indeed a desperate man.

After I'd calmed down a bit, I continued exploration of the kitchen. About two thirds of the way down the left side was the back-entrance door, freshly repaired and repainted, and with a new, solid lock. The contractor hadn't yet dropped the new key off at the motel, as he should have. Making a mental note to check with Sergeant Scarecrow about that, I continued on into the pantry. A lone bulb hung down from the ceiling. I pulled the string and the six by nine shelf-lined room revealed a truly empty larder. Well, I guess I couldn't have expected decades of food to be good anyway.

Somewhat amused with myself, I was about to turn out the light and leave when my eye caught the corner of a board that was sticking out along the back wall. Ever mindful of safety issues, I kicked it back into its proper position. In so doing, I must have jostled a counterweight of some kind for a portion of the back wall began to open wide to reveal a staircase going up to somewhere I wasn't really sure I wanted to go.

"Damn it, Grandfather," I howled. "Why do you do these things to me?"

The pantry light illuminated the first few steps, the remainder being lost in the blackness. I hadn't planned on needing a flashlight. As I went back to the car to retrieve my official Boy Scouts of America lantern, I got this terrible feeling of déjà vu all over again. No no. I surely didn't want another experience like I had the first night. I resolved to this time, keep my reactions under control...I hoped.

Approaching the stairway, the first thing I noticed was that a number of the steps had been recently replaced. Understandable, I guess, in a century-old house. I wondered why they hadn't done the old front porch steps also? The hidden stairway rose in a sharp spiral. Shining the light straight up, it appeared they led all the way to the attic.

"Hmmmm," I said again. "Hmmmm."

I tested each of the old steps carefully. A few of them creaked and groaned pitifully, as I put my full weight on them. Sergeant Scarecrow's brother-in-law, the contractor, must have stumbled upon this passage and taken the initiative to replace some of the steps before somebody got hurt.

CRACK! I clung for dear life to the rickety railing, as my foot broke through one of the steps. Missed that one, I guessed. At the second floor, there was a small landing with rooms on opposite sides; at least, it appeared so from the lights shining under the doors. Cautiously, I put pressure on one of the doors and felt it creak open a few inches. Then I stopped to reflect on what I was doing. The last time I used this flashlight to explore stairs in this house, I found a dead body with lots of blood, nearly broke my pate on a door jam, came close to being changed from a rooster to a hen by a picket-fence gate and ended up in the local clink.

"Now," I softly asked myself, "why the hell am I doing this again?"

All the answers I could come up with contained words like "stupid," "crazy," "buffoon," "dimwit," and well, you get the idea. So, I just picked "all of the above" and continued through the door into what I found was an empty walk-in closet whose doors opened into what was the master bedroom I'd glanced into on the first night, complete with a canopied four-poster with side curtains. Turning back, I crossed over the landing into the other room. It, I surmised, was a servant's quarters; and a female one at that, judging by the pink pastel décor. Why? Why would Grandfather put in a secret stairway with a landing between the master bedroom and... oh. Oh! OH! A big grin spread across my face. "Why Grandfather," I chided softly. "You sly dog, you."

Still chuckling, I continued on with my mission. As I neared the top of the stairway, I could see light streaming in from the attic windows. Topping the last couple of steps, I found myself in a dark corner of the very long attic. At the far end, I could see my brand-new best friend, the gargoyle. Pretty good, I thought, when a guy's best friend is made of concrete and looks like a fugitive from a horror movie.

As I made my way through the dusty doodads, thingamajigs and whatchamacallits, I noticed the large increase in footprints from my last visit up there. Wow. They must have had quite a large crew to have accomplished all this in just one day. I didn't need a flashlight to see that Grandfather's trunk had been moved and new floorboards put in place. All this seemed a little above and beyond the call of duty...but at least I didn't have red paint all over the floor... or blood. I decided, just for argument's sake, to accept for a moment Lieutenant Trevor's assertion that the substance around Grandfather's trunk was in fact red paint, just for argument's sake.

I spent the rest of the afternoon going through history, right there in my own attic. Having been a collector of baseball cards in my youth, I was particularly pleased to find a wonderful bat with "Spaulding League" beautifully burned into it. I guessed it to be just after the turn of the century. "Hmmm," I thought, "wonder what it's worth?" There I go again, putting a price tag on everything. Was it just human nature or greed that kept me putting dollar signs at the end of every thought? Grandfather's warnings about giving in to the lust for wealth crept into my head. Feeling the flush of avarice fade into the shadows of my mind, I leaned the bat up against my new best friend, the gargoyle, and proceeded to finish my inspection of the house.

The bathrooms were five in number, including those for the servants. Quite respectable. Each had a claw-foot bathtub with a free-standing shower curtain surrounding it, obviously a modern addition. Except three of the tubs were missing the curtains. Not a problem, I thought. I could only use one tub at a time anyway.

Finally, I reached the one area of the house I dreaded even more than the attic…the basement. I always did have a basement phobia, probably from watching too many old murder mystery movies as a kid. There was always someone or something untoward hiding in the basement. What would I find? A monster? An alien? Perhaps a race of pygmy-sized cannibals ready to slice and dice my skinny little torso and make me into a mulligan stew. Maybe even some wild-eyed serial killer? Oh, wait. That really was a possibility.

As my hand flicked the basement light switch, I fought the urge to cower back to my Volkswagen and forsake my new home, my new position as upstanding community citizen and even my new treasures—found and unfound. But I could not do that. I could not escape and leave Grandfather in that eternal no man's land. Filled with new resolve, if not courage, I descended the creaking, rickety stairs, wondering with each step if I would suddenly find one foot dangling in midair. However, that did not happen, and I reached the relative safety of the rough concrete. I wondered why, if the contractor who did the repairs was so worried about stairs and flooring, he hadn't checked and replaced some of these. Oh well.

The basement proved to be much less cluttered than the attic. Coming from the Midwest, the first thing I noticed was the furnace…or rather the lack thereof. Although not exactly the tropics, this latitude provided little necessity for external heating even during the coldest months. In Grandfather's day, the beautifully appointed fireplaces provided what heat was necessary on a cold December or January night. I resolved to look into the addition of baseboard heating, somewhere down the road. A quick tour with my official BSA flashlight revealed…well, not a lot. Boxes, bags, tools, and a few unwanted relics, but nothing that would provide a clue to the whereabouts of the missing cadaver I knew I saw in the attic. I looked closely at the picks and shovels to see if they had been used recently, but that didn't appear to be the case.

So. What have I learned today? I learned the dead body hadn't been buried in the basement, and that Grandfather was probably having an affair with his cook. Neither one of those facts got me any closer to Grandfather's treasure or the identity of the mystery cadaver's killer. However, I did also learn that Grandfather was frightened enough of death and what may lay thereafter to leave multiple backup clues to finding his treasure, and most importantly, the purloined cross.

Fact number four was that Sergeant Scarecrow's brother-in-law is a good contractor, and the cleaning crew did an amazing job setting everything back up after the intruders had ransacked the house. That continued to puzzle me. Why would anyone, save for pure meanness, trash a home and not steal anything? To be sure, there were some nice antiques that could probably bring somebody quite a few bucks for booze or drugs. But things that probably should have been stolen under that premise weren't. I suppose they could have been looking for the diary, but the trunk looked like it hadn't been opened since I opened it. They could have been looking for a treasure map, but that didn't seem to fit either. Treasure maps can be hidden anywhere. Not all the pictures had been knocked down, and of those that were, many had their backings still intact. Only some of the books in the library were taken out and scattered. Not all the desk drawers were pulled out. The furniture hadn't been ripped open and searched. Something just didn't set right with the robbery theory. Then...why?

My feet creaked up the basement steps, and I again wondered why the contractor had only fixed the back door, the hidden stairway, and the attic floorboards around Grandfather's trunk, where the red paint had been spilled. I guess I could understand that...maybe. But why just some of the steps? Many of the steps were still in bad shape. Unless...unless those particular steps had red paint on them also. But how could red paint be on a stairway that was clear across the room...one that I, who supposedly spilled the paint, never used?

I got that gut-wrenching feeling again; the one I feel when I really don't want to think something, but I know I will anyway. It was much the same as knowing there might be something wrong with my gall bladder, but forcing myself not to think about it. A big, expensive and dangerous mistake. Reaching the top of the stairs at the kitchen entrance, I crossed over to the new back door and stared out into the fading light at the overgrown lawn with truck ruts where grass used to be.

Forcing my mind back on its track, I ran over my observations again: only selected rickety steps on the hidden stairway had been replaced; none on the basement stairway. Only flooring planks under and around Grandfather's trunk had been replaced. Three of the five shower curtains were missing, but the ground floor two were not. The steps on the stairway would have been replaced, if red paint had been spilled on them, but it wasn't. What then *was* spilled on them to necessitate their immediate replacing? How about blood from a dead body that was wrapped in three shower curtains in a futile attempt to contain it?

I began to shake visibly again. Why couldn't Lieutenant Trevor have been right? Why couldn't I just be paranoid or delusional? I'd even settle for nuts…and that's just what Trevor would think, if I were to go to him, prattling such preposterous possibilities. No. I knew I had to find credible proof that I was neither lying nor looney, concerning my unfortunate encounter with that capricious corpse. Besides, with this latest revelation, I wasn't even sure I could trust Lieutenant Trevor-Tracy-Holmes-Columbo. The workmen were employed by Officer Scarecrow's brother-in-law. Not likely they did the work on their own and not likely Scarecrow's brother-in-law took the initiative. I began to think the city constabulary might be infected with a deadly case of bad copitus. The trashing of my house, then, was not a random act of vandalism or even an attempt to find a legendary treasure map. It was a deliberate attempt to legitimize a cleaning crew coming in that could, without arousing too much suspicion, destroy or hide evidence of a murder.

Oh, boy. Now, what do I do? Couldn't go to the police. I had no idea how widespread their corruption was. FBI? No. They'd lock me up in a looney bin. I decided I'd have to just play out my hand and see where it led me. I hoped it wouldn't be down the garden path to an early grave. Seeing how low the sun had gotten, I checked my cheap electric Timex. Six fifteen. Just time enough to grab a quick bite to eat and perhaps a nap before my midnight rendezvous with destiny…whatever that might be.

My drive to the café was fraught with danger; not because of any nefarious forces, trying to interfere with my life, but because my mind refused to stay focused on my driving. Somehow, by the grace of God, I arrived there unscathed. As I walked in this time, I didn't get the feeling every eye was upon me. That's because the place was practically empty. The crew was different also. Settling into the same booth I'd been in on my previous visits (we are, after all, creatures of habit), I immediately inspected the placemat for any hidden messages, concluding there were none. The waitress, a middle-aged lady with hard eyes and whose disposition seemed more appropriate for a prison matron than a public pleaser, approached me.

"Coffee?" Her smile said she really didn't care but had to ask anyway.

"Yes, please. Black, thank you," I replied in kind. After she plopped the menu down and turned to retrieve my coffee, I regretted my imitation of her very un-Pollyannic mannerism. Not the best way to start out pumping somebody for information. I decided I needed to make amends. As she approached with my coffee, I saw something pinned to her smock that made me believe there was a God and that he, she or it was smiling down upon me.

"Excuse me, miss," I said politely. "That pin you have on—the one of the bear and 'DACC' on it. Is that by any chance a pin from the Des Moines Area Community College Bears?"

She softened just a bit. "Well, ya. My son goes to school there. In Ankeny."

"How delightful. I'm from Des Moines. Been to Ankeny many times."

Her eyes lit up like a Christmas tree, and I swear I could see the cracks in her dour countenance break off and fall away, revealing a genuinely warm person. I thought it remarkably sad that we often allow the pains and sorrows of daily life to plaster over the beauty we really are.

"Oh, really?" she practically squealed. "I haven't been back there for years. My ex lives there, and our son wanted to go to college where his dad did. Tore me up, big time. But I figured the kid had to make his own decisions." Her newly revealed human face turned sad. "God, I miss him so much."

"I can certainly understand that," I comforted her.

She sat down, sucked in a deep breath and pumped a little bravado into herself, forcing a genuine smile. "But at least he comes out here every summer and over spring break." Her tired green eyes began to tear up a little. "Sure do miss the little turd at Christmas, though."

I suppose it's a natural reaction when one human sympathizes with another in distress to reach out both emotionally and physically. That's why when I placed my hand gently atop hers, I knew it had nothing to do with my wanting information from her. It had only to do with my wanting to ease her pain of missing her son. Well, mostly. My gesture did seem to have its intended effect. She smiled again and thanked me. For a moment, I almost abandoned my plot to pump her for information, but I knew I had to. I felt vaguely like a spy who needed to betray someone he'd grown personally fond of.

Since the café was nearly empty, after she brought my food, she sat down, and we chatted for a good two hours. I learned her name was Linda, and she was a transplant from San Diego about five years ago, which may have explained her ignorance of who I was and why I had come to town. She said she had heard of a haunted house, but that she really didn't believe in ghosts. Good thing I didn't tell her of my encounters with Grandfather Hudson. I'm sure she would have considered me a kook, and that might have been the end of my intelligence gathering. But what else I learned from her was very disturbing, to say the least. I asked if she had been working on the afternoon of my first visit there. She said no. The owner had thrown a party for all the employees—on the clock—and brought in a whole new crew.

Three of the Bard's most versatile words popped into my head. "Well, well, well." The plot was indeed thickening. Why, save magnanimity, would a restaurant owner go through the expense of hiring a whole new crew—as small as it was, being only four or five full-time people in such a small establishment—and pay all of the regular employees to attend a party away from the restaurant? The obvious answer was to get them out, so he or she could bring in accomplices to carry out some nefarious plan unseen by the regular crew. That would be, ensuring I would be given the hastily printed placemat to set me on the road to Emerald Bay, as required, and then making sure it disappeared, so I could not show it to the authorities. Somewhat far-fetched but possible, I concluded.

With that disturbing news tucked safely away in my brain, we continued to chat until the clock on the wall chimed 10:00 p.m., and it was closing time. For the first time since my People's Car motored stately into this little seaside city, I felt as though somebody was actually telling me the truth. Before we parted, she gave me her son's name and phone number in Ankeny. I promised to look him up... assuming, that is, I live long enough to get back there.

Too nervous to catch a catnap anyway, I drove to the small beach just down from the cafe, hoping the gentle waves might calm me down. Ya, right. Here I was, the proverbial stranger in a very strange land and about to start dealing with people I was sure were killers even if nobody believed me. I had no weapons, save for a genuine BSA pocket knife and the tire iron from a vintage Volkswagen. I wasn't big and had no formal pugilistic training. Track star? Hell, I couldn't outrun an eighty-year-old pregnant grandmother. That is, of course, unless she had a gun. Fear is a prime motivator. It can give us the mental and physical strength to do things we never dreamed possible. Fear can be healthy. If that be so, then I was a very robust individual who just happened to be shaking like Jell-O in an earthquake. Every time I put all the things I'd found out and seen into my analytical meat grinder, it always came out with the same word to describe my adventure that evening: "Stupid," with a capital "S."

The alarm on my cheap electric Timex was not a loud one... except that night. I had set it to eleven thirty, and when it struck, my heart stopped, my mind froze, and someone pulled the drain plug on my mouth, so the only thing I could spit was dry air. I wondered if that was how soldiers felt, when the hour struck, and they had to charge out into the hell of combat. Perhaps I was to get a small taste of it, one I didn't relish.

The drive to Emerald Bay was a long one; not far, just long. It was a fairly isolated area with few homes, some warehouses and lots of trees. As I neared the drive into the marina, I could barely make out the worn sign, hanging precipitously askew, under a dim streetlamp. My little VW pig bounced and rattled its way down the dirt drive, which was pocked with what I was sure must be bomb craters. More than once, she bottomed out, and I had to gun it to keep from getting hung up. Shadowy fingers in the bright harvest moonlight undulated over the hood, the windshield and me, like the unwelcome caress of a menacing stranger. Why did I feel like I was the victim in an old Charlie Chan murder mystery? The only thing missing was a thick fog and the mournful howl of a hellhound.

It must have been my reference to Charlie Chan that caused me to suddenly reach down and shut off my headlights. Why? Certainly, whomever or whatever awaited me at slip four knew I was coming, and it would probably be beneficial to the investigation into my untimely demise for some bystander to have seen my car bouncing down the driveway, just before midnight on the night I died. But human nature being what it is and my susceptibility to Charlie Chan movies clouding my judgment, I did what my subconscious told me I should do.

Parking my pig off the driveway near some bushes, I got out and froze solid.

"OWHOOOOO!"

No! That was NOT a hound howling. It was not. Please tell me it wasn't a dog's baneful tune.

"OWHOOOOO!"

Yes, it was. Could the night be any more ominous? Could I be given any more reason to jump right back into my car, turn around and flee from what I was sure would be my impending doom? Yes, I could. But I didn't, not even when I looked out toward the ocean and saw the fog beginning to roll in, surrounding everything in its path with all the evils that lurk in a movie about mayhem and murder. No. I had a mission, a mission to save Great-Great-Great-Grandfather Hudson's immortal soul from eternal purgatory. I made a promise and a promise I would keep unto my dying breath, which I hoped wouldn't be that night.

As I made my way toward the water's edge, I could see there were only four slips in the marina at Emerald Bay...and they looked somewhat dilapidated. There were only two boats docked. One in the first slip and one in the last. Slip one had what looked like about a thirty-foot fishing cruiser called The Dutch Shoe. On the opposite end was what I guessed to be about a forty-foot, single-masted sail-boat. The name on the stern was hard to see in the dim light of the lamppost. "R-I-S." "RIS." Just to the left was a picture or a symbol of some kind. It was faded, so I couldn't tell what it was from a distance.

It became clearer as I approached the boat slowly and cautiously. The inner part was round, encompassed by a horizontal envelope that came to a nonsymmetrical point on each end. Oh. Wait. It was an eye. "Eye-ris." "Eye-ris?" "Iris!" Then I knew the party was over because somebody turned out the lights.

# CHAPTER EIGHT

I woke up in the morning with a bell ringing a death knell in my head. What morning? Could have been any morning; I had no idea. I tried to reach up and hold it, but I couldn't. My hands were cuffed to a bunk. I tried to lift my head, but every time I did, the Big Ben in my brain tolled my impending death, should I continue. I did, however, notice that I was wearing different clothing than I had been when the lights went out. Just before slipping back into that middle world between life and death, I beheld an angel in...red?

Yes. Red, I realized, as they...er, I mean she swayed back and forth with the rocking of the boat, not six inches from the tip of my nose, some thirty or more hours later. The red had been the color of her bikini, as she reached over to the far side of the bunk to which I was being shackled. Under normal circumstances, I would have found the experience quite pleasant, even invigorating. However, with a head that felt the size of a watermelon and a face nearly the same color, sweetness was the farthest thing from my mind, as I groaned pitifully and tried to raise my throbbing head, thus bumping into her.

"Oh, Mister Hudson," the angel proclaimed with surprise. "You're alive!"

"Don't get your hopes up," I answered sarcastically. "There's still time."

As she leaned back again, I could see that my angel was none other than...yup, Iris herself. Although "angel" may be too strong a word, she looked nothing like the somewhat matronly motel manager she had portrayed earlier. *Nothing* like it. I looked over at my right hand, cuffed to the bunk railing.

"What's this all about?"

She threw her hands up in front of her. "Hey. Not my idea. They made me do it."

"They, being…?"

"Scott, my husband…unfortunately."

"Haven't had the pleasure yet," I said with thinly disguised sarcasm.

"Oh, sure you have. Wait 'til you meet him. You'll remember."

Some of the fog began clearing from my injured brain.

"What happened?"

"Officially or for real?"

"You decide."

"Well, if you'd died, they were gonna take you out to sea, dump your body and say the boom jibed unexpectedly and knocked you overboard. But since you lived, I can say that Chris hit you way harder than he was supposed to. We thought you were a goner there for a while."

"Supposed to? Huh. Nice company you keep."

"Not a lot of choice when you're married to one of them."

"There's always a choice." I looked down at yet another set of fresh clothes I didn't remember putting on. "How come I keep ending up in different clothes?"

She leaned in as if to keep our dirty little secret from…whom? The fishes?

"Well, Jimmy," she whispered, "you've been in and out of consciousness for three days…and seasick, to boot." She must have sensed my surprise. I remembered nothing after being hit by what I was sure must have been a slow-moving freight train. She continued, "I used to be a nurse's aide back when I was young and single and happy." She grinned. "Besides, it isn't anything I haven't seen before. Nasty lookin'…"

"Gall bladder!" I blurted it out before she could finish.

She laughed. "All right. Gall bladder." This was kind of a quiet, comfortable laugh unlike the knee-slapping belly laughs she and

Kringle had enjoyed at my expense. Well, perhaps she did have a streak of humanity left in her.

Now, Kringle was another matter, if that's the Chris to whom she was referring. His belly may have indeed jiggled like a bowl full of jelly, but his arms approximated the circumference of my thighs with not a lot of jiggle mass. His ho-ho was apparently a mask for his psychopathic tendencies. I would keep that in mind.

The very secretive and elusive "they" say that the mind and body can learn new things, while in a relaxed state of deep sleep. I figured my body subconsciously got used to the constant rocking of the boat; and that, along with the periodic emptying of my stomach and the distraction of a constant headache, served to at least mitigate any seasickness discomfort I ordinarily would have felt. Iris looked at me again with those soft, caring brown eyes. Why the hell did she have to be a crook?

"I would guess you'd be kind of hungry by now, huh?" she said. "I mean, you haven't eaten for three days, only water and a little broth, when I could get it down you."

"So, what kind of rat poison do you use? Does it hurt? Will it kill me quick?" My sarcasm surprised even me. That sounded like something right out of a Mickey Spillane novel. I was kind of proud of that one.

Her eyes looked a little hurt. "Look," she said, "I thought this was a nutty idea in the first place. I tried to talk 'em out of it, but they wouldn't listen."

"You went along with it anyway," I accused.

"What choice did I have? I'm married to one of 'em." Her face became frightened. "You don't know what Scott and Wishy are like when they're mad. They threatened to kill me if I didn't go along. They're capable of anything."

"Wishy? Who the hell is Wishy?"

"Farington. Aloysius Farington."

We stared at each other for a long time until the soft "click" of the main hatch latch echoed through the room like a cannon-shot. She turned away quickly as if to hide her thoughts deep into her mind, away from her husband, who had a bandage over his nose from when I had knocked on Farington's office door. A warm feeling of satisfaction came over me, as he opened the cabin door and walked in. Well, at least I had gotten the first punch in—and a good one it was, too, judging from the looks of the bandage over the fat nose on his fat little face.

"Well, well, Mister Hudson," he said, brushing past his wife. "You're alive. That's a good thing. Wouldn't do to have to feed you to the fishes. Been through too much already, we have."

"You have? *You* have?" I said incredulously.

"But, Mister Hudson, we have been working on this for years now. Put too much into it to screw it up now."

That kind of lit my fire. "Well, excuuuuse me, Scotty boy, but I am the one who's been lied to, made fun of, jailed twice, lured naked into the street, scared half to death by a dead body in my attic, shang-haied and slapped in the back of the head with Paul Bunyan's axe handle! And *you* have been through too much? A little bass-ackwards, aren't we, Scotty boy?"

That actually felt kind of good. After what I'd been through, it felt good to tear into somebody. Didn't make much difference who as long as they deserved it. But his being one of the gang who kid-napped me made it all the sweeter. Well, sweeter for the few seconds it took to say it. Then in my uncharacteristic rage, I lunged at him and almost dislocated my arm, which was still shackled to the bunk.

"Aagh!" The pain was excruciating.

Big Nose chuckled. "Serves you right for what you did to my nose."

I settled back down onto the bed, my arm feeling like it belonged to somebody else...somebody not alive.

"Mister Hudson, we have your diary, only we don't know how to interpret it. We think you do, and so we're willing to enter into a partnership. You decipher the diary, we find the treasure, and we all split it, even shares."

"And if I don't?"

"You become fish food, we eventually figure out the diary and get the treasure anyway."

"Some choice. What makes you think there even is a treasure? Maybe, it's just an old wives' tale."

"Well, Mister Hudson, you've put out a lot of effort chasing an old wives' tale. Besides, we've done our research too. Your ancestor was indeed a pirate—and a successful one too, judging by the house he built. There's been speculation about this for generations. We just decided to do something about it."

The human mind is amazing. It brings up the strangest things at the strangest times. For instance, there are a myriad of phrases used ad nauseam by Hollywood, usually in their low-budget films. "Crazy kid," as the young soldier or cowboy charges out to save the day in the face of enemy fire is one of them. Another popped into my head completely without notice, but I consciously stopped it from escaping my lips. But then I thought, "what the hell?" and blurted it out anyway. "You'll never get away with this." After all, how many more chances would I get to do a movie line like that? "Well," I chuckled to myself later (but not at the time), "none, if I'm dead."

Big Nose laughed. He was on to me. "Come on, Mister Hudson. You can do better than that. That line is as old as the hills."

I resisted the impulse to get into a colloquial urinating contest with him to see who could come up with the most old, worn-out expressions. I think I could have beat him on that, but the sweet sound of salvation cut this contest short.

"Ahoy! Sail ship, *Iris!*" The muffled sound came from a bullhorn. "This is Commander Johnson from the United States Coast Guard! Please heave to. And prepare to be boarded!"

Big Nose turned about the same color as the fresh, white sheets on which I lay. "What the hell do they want?" he exclaimed. "Chris! Get down here!"

Down the ladder lumbered Officer Kringle, not in uniform, of course. Big Nose turned to him. "Cuff him and stuff him!" He paused a moment. "Wow. I've always wanted to say that," he said with a grin. "Keep him quiet, then come up on deck...and bring your badge." With that, he bounded out the cabin door and up the ladder. My new best friend, Officer Ho-Ho, whipped out his handcuff key, grabbed my free arm with an iron grip and came nose to nose with me. There was ice behind his eyes as this bad Santa put the fear of God and everybody else into me.

"Listen to me, Hudson. I will speak very clearly, so there's no misunderstanding. I can snap your scrawny little neck with a flick of a wrist and feed your carcass to the sharks, without the Coast Guard ever having a clue. So, if you wanna play ball, fine; if not, make your peace."

As big as he was, I knew he wasn't just blowing smoke at me. Discretion being the better part of valor, I simply nodded compliance, as he locked both of my arms to the bunk railing at its head. Then, he took out a roll of wide tape—which I assumed he kept handy just for this occasion—and slapped it securely across my mouth. What could I do but to play along and look for a more viable opening?

"Good," he continued. He turned to Iris, handing her a black jack. "Use this, if you have to."

Iris's eyes went wide. I could tell she wasn't used to such tactics. That could be good or bad. That meant she was squeamish about violence; however, it also meant she was not privy to the amount of force necessary to silence a person without killing them...er, him— meaning me. Again, I decided discretion to be the better part of valor.

On deck, we could hear the muffled conversations as the Coast Guard boarded. Commander Johnson said they'd had some trouble with smugglers and somebody had reported a suspicious vessel they needed to check out.

"Would you mind if we had a little look around?" Johnson asked.

"Well, sure; I guess, Commander," Big Nose replied. "But you see, we have a charter business and sometimes cater to clientele that are a little...different."

"I'm a police officer, and I assure you, sir, there are no drugs aboard this vessel," chimed in Officer Claus.

"I didn't say anything about drugs, Officer."

"So you didn't," added Big Nose. "But you must admit that it is the prevalent choice of most smugglers."

"True," agreed Johnson.

At that point, I recognized Farington's mousy little voice. "Commander Johnson, are you by any chance from the San Diego Sector, Squadron One?"

"Yes, sir. That's us."

"Well then, you must know Admiral Johnson. He's a very good friend of mine."

"Yes, sir. I do. He's my dad, and he mentions you often, Mister Farington."

"I'm flattered," came Farington's reply.

"But I'm afraid I must still look around."

I could hear the disappointment in Big Nose's voice. "Of course, Commander. But please be polite to my guests...and discreet."

"Certainly, Captain." He paused. "Lieutenant, take two men and look around...but don't disturb anything."

"Yes, sir," came the reply.

The commander continued. "Captain, SOP states we have the duty to investigate any credible report of smuggling. I'm sure there are no problems here, but I do have to file a report when we get back to port." Then, he added quickly, "And, yes, Mister Farington, my dad is aware of this. In fact, he wrote the directive himself. Captain, I promise, whatever is going on here will stay here, as long as it is legal under international maritime laws. All right?"

"I accept your word, Commander," Big Nose answered.

Now. What happened next, I look back on with very mixed emotions. On one hand, there I was kidnapped by blood-thirsty criminals—even if one was lovely—and handcuffed to a bunk on a sailing yacht, with duct tape over my mouth. But then, on the other hand...

Again, the quiet rattling of the main hatch latch crashed into Iris's ears like the sound of a prison door slamming shut...with her inside. I've heard the phrase, "off like a prom dress" many times, although I never had the chance to test its validity...until now. The desperate shock on Iris's face was priceless, as she used her super human strength to rip my shirt apart, popping all of the buttons, and yank down my parachute pants...a move that under any other circumstances could have totally delighted me. The surprise alone made me struggle and try to voice my opposition.

In the background, I could hear the clump, clump of what we both knew were the highly polished shoes of a Coast Guard officer.

Iris's prom dress was indeed off in a flash, since it consisted of only a bikini, and I calculated her full body weight to be approximately 117.6 pounds, as she landed with full force on my belly, causing a loud but muffled grunt to vibrate through my duct-tape gag.

*Clump, clump, clump.* It reached the cabin door.

I began to grunt and squirm and writhe with fear under the weight of this beautiful, naked woman, which was just what she wanted me to do.

*Knock, knock, knock. Cr...e...a...k...*

Without even glancing down, her hands grasped the back of my head and jerked my face deep into her considerable cleavage, her well-endowed bosom hiding the tape that was covering my mouth. As pleasant as this might have been, it blocked a great deal of my nostrils, and since I have never heard of anyone having the ability to breathe through his eyeballs or ears, my survival instinct kicked into high gear, and my writhing and grunting doubled. Because of the voluminous soft flesh on either side of my head, I couldn't really hear what the Coast Guard officer said, but I would speculate it was something like, "Oh! Excuse me. I didn't mean to interrupt you," as he gazed upon a beautiful naked woman, sitting atop a mostly naked man, whose hands were cuffed to the bunk above his head, which was buried in her large bosom so deeply, the officer couldn't see the man's jaw, or the tape that was covering his mouth. Hey, the commander promised that, what went on aboard the *Iris*, stayed aboard the *Iris*, as long as it wasn't against international maritime law. Since this encounter between two apparently consenting adults onboard a private sailing yacht in international waters didn't seem to fit that criteria, the red-faced officer had no reason to investigate further. Hence, he left us to enjoy our perversions in privacy and peace. And with him went my hopes for salvation.

As the coasties departed, Iris released her iron grip on my head, climbed off and began to put her clothes back on, such as they were. "Whew! That was close," she said with a sigh.

My eyes went wide, not with passionate appreciation for her feminine form, but from my desperate attempts to suck as much air into my oxygen-starved lungs through my uncovered nostrils, as I normally could through an untaped mouth.

"Well," she grinned, mistaking the latter for the former. "Now we've seen each other naked. We're even."

Now I can look back on it with fond appreciation. At the time, I was more concerned with staying alive. After restoring what little modesty I had remaining, she began peeling off the tape from my lips. From the corner of my mouth, there escaped a yowl loud enough that I was sure would bring the coasties racing right back.

"Oh, dear," she exclaimed, with genuine concern. "I'm soooo sorry, Jimmy. I…I've never really done this kind of thing before." She stopped a moment and reflected nostalgically, then continued with a grin. "Well. Not for real anyway."

With that, she retrieved a lemon and a small amount of mineral oil. Squeezing the lemon into the oil, she mixed it up and dabbed it on, as she carefully pulled the tape off my lips. Quite an enigma, this lovely lady who could commit felony kidnapping with such grace and gentility, the victim feels honored to have been chosen.

She stopped abruptly, when she heard the clump, clump, clump of Big Nose's big feet coming down the ladder. He entered and looked at her with surprise.

"What're you doin'?"

"Trying to get this tape off without ripping his lips off with it."

Pushing her out of the way, he grabbed a hold of the tape and gave it a yank, taking several pieces of skin with it. It's hard to describe that pain. Perhaps something akin to being skinned alive, although I've never had that experience either. The words that flew out of my mouth that time are unprintable here.

Big Nose ordered Iris to go get some more clothes on and then turned his attention to me.

"All right, Jimmy boy, let's get started. We're out in the middle of the Pacific Ocean. There are four of us and one of you. We have guns, and you don't. We have all the cards. Now, you can play ball with us or sleep with the fishes. I'm going to take these cuffs off, and you are going to behave. Capisci?"

"Well," I said, "better half a loaf than a burning bridge...or something like that."

"Good. Now, let's get you started making all of us fabulously wealthy." With that, he unhooked the cuffs and retrieved Grandfather's diary from a drawer under the bunk.

For the next day and a half, I poured over the book, trying to memorize every passage I thought might be important. The only time I was allowed to be alone was in the head. All the men were armed, and all the radios and emergency flares were under lock and key. Iris refused to carry a gun. Occasionally, I would stroll on deck for some fresh air. I began to understand the lure of the open sea.

Funny sometimes how desolation can be so beautiful and even alluring, like the beautiful face of a dangerous woman. The aloneness can be so liberating...or so stifling. Even with others aboard and even if those others are not your friends, it gives one a sense that all you have are each other...and God.

The night before the storm hit was one of those magical evenings one sees only in old movies. Winds were calm, the stars played about the dark sky and the moon...oh, yes, the moon; it hung so huge upon the water at the edge of the world, I thought sure we would slide right off. The only thing missing was a snifter of cognac and a beautiful woman...uh, one who isn't a crook.

Well, sometimes, when close enough comes along, you've just got to jump on it. I felt the heat, as she came up beside me.

"Some people still think it's flat."

"Huh?"

"The earth. Some people still believe the earth is flat. They even have their own club."

I chuckled. "Ya. So I've heard. Looks flat to me."

"Things aren't always how they look."

"Ya. I'm kind of counting on that now."

"Me too."

"So, how did a woman with your obvious intelligence and beauty ever end up running a fleabag motel in bum intercourse, California?"

"Fleabag?"

"Well, OK, I'm sorry, it's actually very clean.

She seemed to accept that. "But really," I continued. "How did you get mixed up with these creeps?"

"Young and dumb," she answered. "Nursing wasn't all I thought it would be. Got restless. Scott was a successful businessman. Had this yacht, a nice home, and backstage access to the best concerts. What red-blooded American girl wouldn't jump at that chance?" She shook her head just a bit. "Huh. I guess young and dumb is putting it mildly. Anyway, things were fine for a while until the markets tanked, and the money dried up. He started taking on charters, and I got a job in the motel. Bought it on a land contract when the owners retired."

"No kids?" I asked. She shook her head, a hurt coming over her face. "What happened to the town? Looks like it was quite prosperous at one time."

"Freeway got routed around us. Tourist trade went around us too. We don't have much of a coast. All rocks. What you saw in town, down from the Jolly Roger, and by the marina is just about all there is that's accessible. No self-respecting resort chain wants to build where their guests have to take an elevator down to a beach they can barely sunbathe on without getting their feet wet."

"So, they dreamed up this cockamamie scheme to lure tourists into town with wild stories of haunted houses and buried treasure."

"Well, sort of."

"OK. Spill it."

"That's what Gary, Wishy, Chris, and a few others told the town council anyway. They needed a cover. So they cooked the whole thing up to grab a few headlines, make it look legit and then let the whole thing quietly die."

"Yes," I interrupted. "And me with it."

She frowned. "Oh, no. The intention never was to harm you."

"What made them think it would work anyway?"

"They didn't. They just used it as a ploy to get to you, and the rest of the town was too dumb to realize just how bad the plan was."

"Did the whole town know about this? Seemed like it."

She shook her pretty head. "No. Only the town council, the mayor, and about ten or so members of a committee they set up." She paused a moment. "Well, of course, everybody knew about your pirate ancestor and heard the stories about maps and buried treasure. That's been around forever. But only a couple dozen people knew about this."

"But wouldn't *somebody* balk at even a phony kidnapping? That's a federal offense."

"As far as anybody else knew, you were in on it."

"How unbelievably stupid," I said with astonishment.

She grinned. "But you *are* here, aren't you?"

Guess I couldn't argue with her there. So, it seemed I was the victim of a bad plan gone good. It occurred to me that I might be cultivating an ally here in little Iris. I decided to add a little fertilizer.

"He doesn't deserve you," I told her, staring right into those big, beautiful brown eyes.

"You're right," she answered. "He doesn't." With that, she got up and turned toward the hatch. "Come on. We gotta hook you up for the night."

"What for? It's not like I've got anywhere to go, and I'm not about to swim a hundred miles to shore."

"Ya. I know," she answered, "but Scott will have a cow, if I don't."

Perhaps I could make a little hay here too. "He hits you, doesn't he?"

Her silence chilled the warm sea air, and her gaze travelled through a time/space continuum to a place she didn't want to be; a place whose memory was far more painful than the bruises she suffered. Wrenching herself back from this abyss, she spoke curtly, "Come on. Let's go."

I decided I had pushed the subject just far enough to get her thinking about it. Any more and she might have become defensive toward me. Didn't want that.

Stuff happens. Storms happen. Sometimes, they happen faster than our brains can comprehend. For instance, I didn't know why I was suddenly hanging by my handcuffed arm to a bunk that had been horizontal to the earth, but now was vertical. Just about the time I figured it out, I was thrown back onto the bunk, as the Iris rolled her herself back and toward the opposite side. Unsecured crap flew all over the place. Panic? Yes. I panicked, as a water pitcher flew past my head.

"Iris! Iris!" I screamed at the top of my lungs, which for the moment were free of seawater, and that's how I wanted to keep them. "Iris, cut me loose! I...ris!"

Through all the noise, I couldn't hear her dainty steps making their way down the ladder and into the cabin. Stumbling like a drunkard, she made her way over to me with the handcuff key in one hand and a life jacket in the other.

"Here!" she shouted. "Put this on! Scott needs you up on deck! He couldn't get the engine started! Chris got hit by the boom! He's out cold! Wishy's sick in his cabin! Scott needs your help!"

I must've indeed acquired those most elusive sea legs for the violent rocking of the boat had no effect on my stomach. Or perhaps it was fear that had steeled my innards against their normal aversion to such things. I suspect the latter. Once free of my tether, I followed Iris up the ladder. What greeted us on deck was something right out of *MOBY DICK* or *TWO YEARS BEFORE THE MAST*, both of which I had read so often as a boy, I could practically quote chapter and verse.

At this point, I should say that before I found out my heart belonged to the sea but my stomach did not, I had studied sailing, thus becoming somewhat familiar with its terms and actions...at least, on paper. Therefore, I could describe the situation in which we were mired as dire. The on-deck work lights bathed this surreal scene in a ghostly glow. Big Nose was at the helm in the cockpit, fighting waves and wind for life and limb...ours. Officer Kringle lay nearby, facedown, out cold…or dead. Luckily for him, his safety line was still attached to the runner that went from bow to stern; otherwise, he'd be fish food already.

Iris turned to me and shouted over the noise. "The traveler cleat ripped off. I couldn't hold the boom sheet. We jibed, and the boom hit Chris in the head!"

I could see the boom swinging wildly. The cleat was still tethered to the end of the rope—called a sheet in sailing lingo—that controlled the swinging of the boom. It had ripped up from the channel that ran from port to starboard (left to right) called a traveler. There was no way in hell it could be fixed in this storm, so I had to figure out a way of securing it to something solid enough to hold it. I remembered seeing a small winch at the stern. I figured that if I could make my way back to it and release the brake, I could pull enough slack out to hook the boom or at least the wayward traveler cleat; then make my way back to the winch and reel it tight.

Clipping a safety rope to my life jacket, I hooked the other end over the safety line and fought my way on deck toward the winch. Fresh rain mingled with seawater to periodically pelt my face with a sting that felt like a thousand mosquitos sucking out my lifeblood. Several times, my hard-soled shoes caused me to slip and nearly be washed overboard were it not for the safety line. However, I figured in seas this rough, my life jacket would only serve to delay the inevitable, since there would be little chance in Hades I'd be found. Reaching the winch, I released the brake and began pulling out the nylon rope. After what seemed like the eleven-millionth time my hard-soled shoes went surfing on the waves that rolled over the deck, I paused long enough to take them off and throw them overboard. Grabbing on to anything I could find, I got to the end of the boom as it swung back and forth, the broken cleat flying in the wind. I figured trying to grab the boom itself would only put me down, as it did Kringle, so I fished the air for the flying cleat. *Wham!* It smacked right into my outstretched arm and wound around it, jerking me toward the blackness of death that eagerly awaited any victim unlucky enough to be swept overboard on such a night. With my other hand, I slammed the winch's hook over the cleat, catching an open space where the hook would not slide off. Fighting not to be pulled overboard by the swinging boom, I disengaged my arm from the sheet and crawled, hand over shaking hand, back to the winch. Slamming the brake back on, I reeled the boom sheet in, keeping one eye on the boom and one on Big Nose. After it was in the proper position, he nodded to me and yelled something unintelligible, then nodded for Iris to reef (or shorten down) the main sail. She made her way to the mast end of the boom. Wow, I thought. One gutsy lady. But then, we never know of what we are capable until we have no choice. Do it or die. Pretty good incentive, I'd say. It looked as if things had come back under control again. The boom was secured at the correct angle, and Big Nose was tying the rudder in the proper opposite position to counteract the wind, essentially stopping the boat to keep it more stable in the storm. We were, in sailing jargon, hove to. The next monumental task—and they all seem to be monumental in a storm—was to check the condition of Officer Kringle. God forgive me please, but considering the circumstances and what he'd already put me through, I would not have shed a lot of tears had the man expired. I look back on it still with mixed emotions. To wish a person dead is tantamount to killing him/her one's self…even without the possibility of criminal prosecution. It just goes against my nature. On the other hand…

At that instant, a huge wave washed over the boat, knocking both of us down and snapping the safety line at the bow, sending Iris flying toward the open sea, her safety clip sliding off the line's ragged end. I launched myself, as she landed near the starboard gunwale, my own safety rope trailing behind and the clip getting very near the same jagged end of the line. Grabbing the safety line with my right hand, I wrapped it around as many times as I could. My left hand shot out to catch Iris, and I felt it close around a strap of her life jacket. I could hear her screaming.

# The storm

"Jimmy! Jimmy! Help me! Don't let me die! Jimmy! Please!"

I have read that most winners of medals in combat don't consider themselves heroes. In fact, many feel as if they don't deserve such recognition because they were only doing their job and helping keep their buddies alive. I guess I got a miniscule taste of how they feel because all I could think was I can't let her die. She's a human being, and as such, I have an obligation to do everything I can to help her stay alive.

So, there I was, this nerdy, sometimes-substitute teacher from Podunk, Iowa lying facedown on the deck of a forty-odd-foot sloop that was pitching and rolling wildly in the middle of the night in the middle of a howling gale. One hand was clinging to a beautiful woman who was begging me to save her and the other hand trying to hold on to the thin line of nylon rope that was keeping us both alive. What the hell had I gotten myself into?

As I feared, the worst began to happen, as the wet nylon safety line began slipping through my grip. I turned my head back to Iris. The fear in her eyes was indescribable, perhaps akin to that of a condemned person or an enemy soldier about to die. With every fiber of my being, I concentrated on holding on to that rope. Knowing that my only salvation would be to let Iris die and grasp the line with both hands. But I could not do that, I just couldn't. We would either live together or die together. I now imagine that to be similar to the camaraderie soldiers feel on the battlefield.

Putting my head down on the deck, I mumbled some not-so-silent prayers to God (again, whomever he, she or it may be) to give me the strength I needed to hang on. With every roll of the ship, I felt the line slip a little more. Panic set in, and to my own shame, the thought of actually letting Iris die raced through my mind, powered I surmised by the survival instinct we all have. Through my mind is accurate because I fought that instinct with everything I had.

The rope suddenly went slack, and thinking the line had now snapped at the stern, I mentally prepared myself to die; to not fight the sensation, as the cold seawater filled my lungs. This was it. Well, at least Iris and I would die in each other's arms. What is it about the human psyche that allows a man to smile at such a time? But I did smile at how corny that thought sounded. Perhaps, I reasoned, Iris and I could laugh about it in the afterlife...if there is one.

But then at the same time, I felt another sensation. A vice had clamped around my right arm and was pulling it with such force; I thought sure it would separate from my shoulder, and I would die with only one arm. What a dumb thing to worry about before entering into the underworld. I turned my head to see the vice. The big, ugly, beautiful face of Officer Kringle was staring back at me, his hand clasped around my arm, and his toes hooked over the edge of the cockpit.

"Uh-uh, Hudson!" he shouted. "You ain't goin' nowhere, 'til we find that treasure!"

How could I have not cared if Kringle died or not? This man, who had nearly killed me with a black jack—albeit not on purpose—was risking his own life to save mine and Iris's, his motivation notwithstanding. Humans are strange creatures indeed. About that time, I didn't care if he were Attila the Hun. Had I been able, I would have kissed him like I did that lovely gargoyle…well, minus the tongue, I guess. I strengthened my grip on Iris, as Kringle hauled us to safety.

It wasn't long after that the storm began to subside, and we were able to make our way below deck. Once he was confident the storm was no longer a threat, Big Nose deployed a sea anchor to counteract drifting from the waves. In addition to being hove to, that allowed him to get a few hours of much-needed rest…along with the rest of us. Wishy? He slept in the head, next to the toilet he'd been hugging all through the ordeal. Apparently, some dryland sailors never do get their sea legs.

# CHAPTER NINE

The next day (whatever day it was; I had long since lost track) dawned beautiful and warm. A light breeze ruffled the sails, teasing them incessantly with the promise to fulfill their ultimate desire to surge forward, only to run away, laughing and mocking them for their gullibility. Hmmm. Vaguely reminiscent of my old girlfriends, I thought. Wishy was still green from the night before; Big Nose was at the helm, and Kringle was recovering from the smacking he got when that wayward boom tried to lobotomize him, assuming there was something there to lobotomize.

Iris joined me, sitting on a bench near the stern; she was carrying a pair of deck shoes. "Here," she said. "Put these on. Those damn street shoes almost got you killed last night. Wonder you didn't surf right overboard." Her eyes softened, as she continued. "Jimmy, I haven't had a chance to properly thank you for saving my life last night."

"I couldn't just let you drown," I replied.

"Why not? You'd have one less of us to worry about."

"I guess I just don't have it in me to let somebody die, if there's a chance I can help save them."

Impulse is an interesting thing. Do we act because some unseen entity takes temporary control of our actions? Or could it be that our conscious state temporarily lowers the walls that keep our hidden inner feelings from manifesting themselves? I kind of thought it was the latter, when her hands cupped my face, and her lips smashed into mine…forever, or so it seemed. There was something about that kiss that carried it well beyond "thank you." So now, I have a beautiful, married woman throwing a lip-lock on me with her husband not fifteen feet from us…and by the way, wearing a gun. My, oh my. Des Moines was never like this.

As her lips began to part from mine, I instinctively followed her. I didn't want it to stop, and when she pulled away, I felt almost like I had violated some kind of law against enjoying the kiss of a married woman, even though it was she who did the kissing. Perhaps it was so enjoyable because for just that one brief eternity, there was no boat, no treasure, no danger; and she was not a married kidnapper, and we were alone. Sometimes, it's tough being an incurable romantic. Oh well.

After that awkward moment when we both realized what had happened, I bent down and put my new deck shoes on.

"We reach the island tomorrow," she said.

"Oh? And what island is that?" I baited her.

"You know very well which one. Cocos Island."

I gave her my dumbest look—which is easy for me—and shrugged my shoulders.

"Jimmy," she answered with a knowing look, "in the private reading room at the library, you plotted five degrees, fifty-three minutes, north and eighty-seven degrees, six minutes, west. Approximately three hundred and forty nautical miles off the coast of Costa Rica. *That* is Cocos Island, said to be the hiding place of the fabulous treasure of Lima, Peru." She let that sink in a moment. "Need I go on?"

I thought back to that occasion. My back was to the door, so they couldn't have watched me from there. Ah! The colored glass dome on the wall next to the PA speaker. Must have had some kind of hidden camera inside of it. Technology is remarkable.

"So, what else do you know about me…besides my gall bladder scar, that is?"

"A lot," she replied, pausing a moment. "Your mom and dad both teachers. You followed dutifully in their footsteps. Good grades in college, but nothing to write home about." The more she talked, the bigger my eyes got. "Two girlfriends. One who loved you, and you left her for the one you loved…who left you." She gave me that quizzical look of "do you want to hear more?"

"OK," I told her. "You can stop now. You've gone too far already. How'd you find all that out anyway?"

She smiled. "Chris is a cop, remember? He knows people who have access to information." These revelations served a reminder to my errant romanticism of just what and with whom I was dealing. Again, I let my heart overwhelm my head. I've got to stop doing that too.

We reached our island of dreams—or nightmares—about dusk the next day. Big Nose decided to give the north end a wide birth, to reduce the risk of the park rangers, who live on the island, seeing our approaching vessel and wanting to track us. We anchored about two-thirds of the way from East Point to Dampier Head behind a small rock, barely big enough to hide us. That night, I was again locked to my bunk. All the windows were covered, and the deck work lights kept off all night. As Iris leaned over to lock my handcuff, I whispered to her. "They're going to kill me, you know." This startled her.

"No, they're not," she replied. "They just want a cut of the treasure. That's all."

"There's more at stake for them than that…and you know it."

"What d'ya mean?"

"That dead body in the attic of my house behind the trunk. I'm guessing that was Mister Jasper, the agent from the trust company."

"Don't be silly. You saw the mannequin yourself with the red paint all over it."

"I saw a dead body with blood all over it. That's what I saw." She got very serious, as I continued to speculate. "Jasper found out about their plan, and when he wouldn't go along with it, they killed him. Now, shock set in on her face. "Why up in the attic, I don't know. But I know a dead body when I see one."

Iris didn't say anything after that, but that night, she and Big Nose got into a terrible, if somewhat muted argument. It became clear to me that Big Nose, Wishy and Kringle had indeed murdered Mister Jasper; and that Iris, although guilty of other serious crimes, was not an accessory to murder. I slept fitfully.

Just as dawn was cracking the next morning, I was awakened by the same sight I'd seen when I first woke up in that bunk. Under other circumstances, quite delightful. This time, Iris was quietly removing my handcuffs. She looked frightened but determined, as she cautioned me to be quiet. Ever so slowly, we made our way up the ladder and on deck. In the yellow morning sun, I could see one lone seagull circling the yacht. It had strange markings on its dirty white feathers that resembled a black belt around its girth.

"Go on," Iris whispered, nudging me in the back. Taking careful steps so as not to wake the others below, she led me to where a small, inflatable lifeboat was bobbing up and down next to the sloop's hull. It was one I had looked upon with covetous eyes several times, just waiting for my opportunity. However, stealing a lifeboat in the middle of the Pacific Ocean would have been folly indeed.

"There's a small coconut grove a couple hundred yards up the coast," she continued in a quiet voice. "You can land there, hide the lifeboat and try to make your way to the ranger station on the other side of the island."

"No," I insisted. "You're coming with me."

"I can't. I'll only slow you down. I'm not a climber. I'm afraid of heights." She grinned.

"But you can't stay here. They'll kill you."

"No. Not if you hit me hard enough to knock me out. I'll tell them you had to puke, so I took you up on deck, and you jumped me."

"Iris, I can't do that."

"I'll be fine, Jimmy. You have to, or they'll suspect something."

I've never hit a woman, not even in play. But sometimes we have to do bad things for good reasons. This time, it was I who took her face in my hands, smashing my lips to hers…just before my fist to her jaw. A grunt escaped her lips, as her body crumpled. Fearing her head might hit the deck too hard, I reached out and grabbed her tank top. That did the trick, slowing her descent down enough for her hair to cushion her connection with the deck. I looked down at the ripped tank top, still gipped tightly in my hand. Well, if Big Nose had any doubts that I was a woman-beating animal to rival him, they would vanish now.

Iris's grunt and her body hitting the deck were bound to arouse the others below, so I immediately threw her top down and clambered over the side into the boat. The sea being relatively calm, I began to row around the rock toward shore. My mind took me back to those Viking films wherein the rowers had to row for all their worth to save their own necks. Now, I could identify. Looking up during a backstroke, I saw Big Nose on the deck with a gun. I groaned and pulled like there was no tomorrow, which was a possibility.

I looked up again. Big Nose was just drawing a bead on me. Well, probably not me; he didn't want to kill the golden goose. But if he popped my inflated lifeboat, he'd have at least a chance to get to me before the sharks that permeated this area found a tasty little corn-fed snack.

## *My friend; my saving grace; my protector*

Before he could fire, a seagull—which appeared to be the same one that was circling around earlier—began a dive-bombing campaign, the likes of which I had never before seen. First, the gull would swoop in from one direction, digging his talons into Big Nose's gun hand, just enough to hurt. Then it would fly off, bank around and do it again from the opposite direction. I swear that bird had to have been the reincarnation of Major Dick Bong, America's World War Two Ace of Aces. Glad I wasn't on the receiving end of that attack.

At least it gave me the chance to pull away out of Big Nose's effective range. With both the yacht and the lifeboat rocking on the waves, chances were slim he'd be able to hit me with a pistol shot. The last I remember seeing Kringle and Wishy had come up on deck and were chasing that lovely little avian away. Oh well. It accomplished its mission. Upon later reflection, I reasoned Big Nose may have had a food smell on his hands, and the gull was hungry. Sounded good to me anyway.

Glancing behind me, I saw the coconut trees Iris had told me about and adjusted my course accordingly. I was sure Big Nose and the gang would be launching a dinghy to give chase, so I didn't waste time looking back again. I just rowed for all I was worth. In fact, I didn't realize how close I was until my oars hit bottom. Jumping out, I hauled the inflated boat up onto what little beach there was and looked back out to sea. They were headed out behind me in a motorized dinghy. Well, no use trying to hide my little dinghy. Just run like hell. But where? Up and down the beach was useless. Both directions deteriorated into rocks and sheer cliffs. That left only straight inland.

And run I did. But not before checking the dinghy for survival supplies. I found precious little: a few wafers, some water and some fishing gear, but no emergency flare. Big Nose had been very thorough in keeping any sort of signaling device out of my hands. I used some of the line to tie the bottles around me the best I could, stuffed the wafers into my shorts pocket and set off at a dead run toward what looked to me like Mount Everest. I cursed myself for not ordering that "How to be a Mountain Goat in Ten Easy Lessons" course that was offered at the back of nearly every comic book I'd ever bought. Oh well. OJT, I guess.

Luckily, I found a trail...of sorts. I guessed it was used maybe by pigs or deer, which the books say inhabit the island. Fear can change a man. I was hoping it would change me into a mountain goat. It could have because my hands didn't merely grip the rocks and brushes that afforded marginal support on my steep climb; they clamped down hard and held fast like a super glue.

Time and distance get distorted with fear. By the time I needed a rest, I looked up and saw I was nearly halfway to the top. Looking back, I saw the dinghy just making landfall. Much to my surprise and dismay, Iris was with them. During my brief respite at the mid-point, the reality of my surroundings flowed over me...literally. The heat and humidity were stifling. Sweat ran down my face and body like a waterfall. This island was home to at least a gazillion species of mosquitoes, flies, gnats, spiders, and assorted other vermin that will survive long after man has succeeded in exterminating himself; and I swear every one of them was after my blood.

Seeing that the wrecking crew below had beached and was headed inland, I resumed my flight up these tropical Alps. Often, I had to use a vine or root that was protruding from a rocky crevasse to pull myself up to the next level, an act that I'm sure would have given any conscientious rock climber conniption fits. But when one is running from killers, that's an acceptable risk.

After climbing for what seemed like hours, I found myself... well, lost. I had reached a plateau of sorts. Looking around through sweat-stained eyes, I saw trees and bushes and rocks and birds and... more of the same. Two things I knew for sure: I couldn't get completely lost forever on an island two miles wide and six miles long, so I was bound to find a coast... eventually. Secondly, I would eventually find the ranger station all the books said was on the island. That is, if I didn't break a leg, arm or neck climbing around on the rocks and tramping through the dense jungle, which was full of all kinds of nasty things like poisonous spiders, snakes, and feral pigs, to name but a few. But these were not your ordinary, everyday household, garden variety, farmland animals. Oh no. These were descendants of animals brought here by sailors over the last two hundred years or so. Some escaped, and some were released. Over the generations, their domestication was bred out of them, and they reverted back to their primordial instincts, becoming hunters and killers in order to survive. This is as opposed to man who sometimes kills just for the fun of it. I wonder, who is the real animal?

However, having said all that, the fact that an animal was only trying to kill me for food gave me no comfort at all, as the largest, meanest, ugliest monster quadruped on the face of the earth charged out across a small clearing, baring his fangs and uttering a sound that could only have originated deep in the bowels of hell itself. I stood there, frozen with fear and once again preparing to meet my maker. What did I have? A pocket knife, a few fishhooks and some water bottles. I grabbed one of the bottles and threw it at him, hoping at least to slow his advance long enough for me to find a tree. Wrong on both points. All I saw was a mass of dirty hair blocking out the sweltering sun, as he knocked me backwards, his eyes burning with the fires of hell, and his massive jaws seeking the vein of life in my neck. The prophetic image of the wolf painting that scared the bejee-zus out of me in the hallway of Grandfather's house flashed through my mind, as my arm shot up to block him, his jaws closing over it. I could smell the stench of yesterday's kill on his breath and in his saliva, as it dropped in puddles on my chest and face.

## Charge of the wild boar

We both let out a scream of terror and pain. Then, there was blood everywhere. Blood shot out in spurts from a heart that soon would no longer beat. His massive body twisted wildly and collapsed on top of me still. Blood ran all over me, but it wasn't mine.

With a grunt, I rolled the animal's dead carcass off me. Two crude but obviously effective arrows protruded from his throat and his heart. Astonished, I looked around to find my savior in the form of a young lad of about fifteen or so, and I guessed of Latino descent. His dark skin covered a bright face with high cheekbones and sparkling eyes; it was all wrapped up jet-black hair that had been crudely cut. He wore the remnants of green Bermuda shorts, a blue tank top, ragged white tennis shoes and a grin of satisfaction that ran from ear to ear.

"That was close, senor," he said in a thick Latino accent. "There are many here like him, but he was the worst. I had a lucky shot with the first arrow. Pure skill with the second."

Still stunned speechless, it took me a minute to find my voice, blurting out the first thought that ran through my befuddled mind. "Who the hell are you?" Now, my first words should have been of undying gratitude, but at such times as these, polite protocol seems to fly out the window.

"I am Juan Carlos Manuel Fernando Moralez, senor," he said with a smile and a slight bow. My sense of propriety returning, I matched his bow and extended my hand.

"James Bartholomew Hudson the Third," I said, as he took my hand. "And I am forever in your debt, sir."

"Think nothing of it, Senor Hudson," he replied. "We are both fugitives on the run. We must stick together."

I wondered for a moment what he was running from. Moreover, how did he know I was running from somebody? I looked at him quizzically. He saw my confusion.

"In due time, Senor Hudson," he offered. "But first, we have to get this body out of sight in case the rangers find it before the scavengers do and discover two arrow holes in it."

"Rangers? Oh no. We need to find the park rangers. Those kidnappers are still after me. We have to find them as soon as possible," I countered.

"Senor Hudson," he queried, "do you have a passport? A visa?" I shook my head. He continued. "Both of these are required to be here, senor. You would be arrested immediately and sent to the mainland on the next ship…in about a month." I just stared at him, as he let even more air out of my rescue bubble. "In addition to that, senor, they may charge you with treasure hunting, which is illegal on this island. Even if you were to be exonerated, just getting through the legal process could take a year or more. Do you have that amount of time to spend in a Costa Rican jail, senor?" I hesitated.

"Come on," I said, grabbing the beast's hind leg and dragging it toward a pile of deadfall brush. "Let's get this out of here before Big Nose and Santa Claus show up."

"Who, senor?"

"The ones who are chasing me. Long story. I'll tell you later."

No sooner had we finished hiding the monster's carcass, when around the corner on the opposite side of the clearing trudged Big Nose, Kringle and Iris. Wishy was nowhere to be seen.

"Come quickly, senor," Juan whispered hoarsely.

We started off at a dead run. Well, as much as I could, after having rowed for my life, climbed a mountain halfway to the clouds and wrestled with a monster. Still, the survival instinct kicked in again. Behind me, I could hear the "pop" of a small pistol just after the bullet whizzed by my ear so close, I swear I could feel the breeze. Upon later reflection, the fact that one of them would take a chance on killing me before finding the treasure and in the process alerting the park rangers that their island had been invaded puzzled and disturbed me. That might mean their main intent had mutated from treasure hunting to keeping Mister Jasper's murder a secret; and that would mean eliminating me and possibly Iris too. I wanted to get as far away from them as I could.

Following Juan was not easy. He obviously knew where he was going and how to get there without breaking any bones. I, on the other hand, did not. The arm on which the beast had tried to snack began to throb rhythmically with every beat of my racing heart. The teeth had not had the opportunity to puncture the skin, so infection probably would not be a problem. But it was beginning to bruise and turn all kinds of pretty colors. I decided I would have to emulate the professional football players I had idolized as a young boy and just work through the pain. Of course, running in fear of my mortal life from killers bent on denying it to me helped a lot too.

Glancing back at every opportunity, I saw that Iris hadn't lied to me about one thing anyway; she was not a climber. Every time I looked, she appeared to be lagging farther behind with Big Nose yelling at her to keep up. Perhaps she was falling back in hopes of escaping from them at the first opportunity. But considering the ordeal I had just gone through, I thought that would be a very bad idea. After dodging branches, stumbling on rocks and swatting mosquitoes the size of dive bombers for what seemed like hours—but was probably only a few minutes—Juan thought it safe enough to stop on a small plateau to rest. Looking back, we could see Big Nose, Kringle and Iris several hundred yards behind us, talking furiously to a couple of park rangers. I guess the rangers weren't buying whatever cock-and-bull story they were being handed, for soon the rangers drew their weapons and placed the trio under arrest. I smiled because it couldn't happen to a couple of nicer guys, and it would also ensure Iris's safety from the dangerous animals that would seek to harm her—four-legged and two-legged.

"Guess we don't have to worry about them anymore, Juan." He was not smiling.

"Yes, senor," he answered. "But I worry that they will tell the rangers we are here, and that would be very bad for us, senor."

I chuckled. "I doubt that, Juan," I reassured him. "Those three are in deep dodo enough as it is. I doubt they're going to be telling the rangers that they're actually treasure hunters, chasing a guy they kidnapped, so they can kill him. No. I think our secret is safe…for now."

This seemed to allay Juan's fears a bit, and he acknowledged with a nod and a slight smile. "True, senor. That makes sense. Treasure hunting is illegal here."

"So is murder." I smiled back, then added, "I hope." He laughed.

"Come, senor. We have a many hills to climb before nightfall." With that, he turned and started off again at a more leisurely pace… thank God.

We arrived at the foot of a waterfall—one of over two hundred that cascade abundant rainfall down precipitous cliffs to eventually join their briny cousin in the Pacific Ocean, just as the sun was beginning to set. The approach to the small pool formed by the constant barrage of water was mostly rocky and treacherous. Juan was careful to cover any footprints we made in the surrounding soil. Normally, huge amounts of rainfall would eradicate them; but this being the dry season, he had to be more careful of detection although he told me that he'd never seen rangers ambitious or stupid enough to venture into such territory without compelling cause.

Edging under the waterfall, we entered a cave that I later discovered ran a hundred or so yards into the hillside with several offshoots of varying depths. As we entered beyond the point where outside light filtered in, Juan picked up an old kerosene lantern, fished in his pocket for a lighter, fired up the lantern, and we proceeded deeper into the cavern. Again, I seemed to be transported through time to an era... well, actually, many eras. Arranged about the far end were a myriad of objects that Juan had scavenged about the island; objects left behind mostly by unlucky treasure hunters who, giving up in disgust, simply dropped everything and retreated back to the safety and comfort of civilization such as it was. There were picks, shovels, axes, several coils of ropes of all types, including nylon; there were three or four cot frames whose canvass has long since rotted off. On one of these, Juan had constructed a makeshift hammock, using some of the discarded nylon rope. There were a couple of camp cookstoves that he had converted from propane to wood. One of them had been used extensively. A wide assortment of plates, cups, and tableware sat on a ledge in one corner. In one of the small side rooms, he stacked dried driftwood, gleaned off the beaches at night, to use for cooking and occasionally for warmth—but not often, at this latitude. His kitchen, which contained the fire pit, was around a corner in one of the anterooms, so light from the fire did not project directly out the cave entrance. A small alcove provided a relatively cool area to be his refrigerator. All in all, this remarkable young man who had saved me from becoming animal feed had fashioned a right comfortable apartment for himself; and now, I would be his new roommate for a while anyway.

After a fine meal of roast pig—slain that very morning—and fresh fruit, Juan expertly fashioned another cot for me, using one of the discarded frames and nylon rope. As he worked, we talked. I wanted to know more about this possible new ally I had found or who had found me.

"So, Juan," I asked, "what brought you here to this God-forsaken island?"

"A yacht, senor. Like you." He grinned.

"They abandoned you?"

"No, senor. I jumped ship. Like you. Nearly a year ago now."

"Why? Aren't your parents worried about you?"

His demeanor changed. "No. Mi madre y mi padre están muertos." He hesitated to translate in his head. "They are dead, senor. My mother died when I was born, and my father died at sea, when his fishing boat was caught in a storm. I was sent to an orphanage." His eyes narrowed, and the pain fairly dripped from his gaze. "A horrible place, senor. The things that went on there are too much even to speak of. I still have... *pesadillas*." He thought again. "How you say it...nightmares."

"Wow. I'm so sorry to hear that, Juan," I said. "So, you shipped aboard a yacht?"

He chuckled. "No, senor. I stowed away. When I escaped from the orphanage, I didn't care where I ended up as long as it was not back in that small corner of hell. When I got to the beach, I saw a large yacht with nobody around. So, I climbed aboard and hid in a gear locker."

"The yacht was headed here?"

"Si. They were *Genta rica*...rich people with nothing better to do than cruise around the world, drinking and having parties. They thought they could slip onto the island and hunt for the treasure without being caught. Or maybe because they were rich, they thought it was their privilege to do that. I don't know. But they turned out to be not much better than the animals that ran the orphanage. So, at the first opportunity, I stole what supplies I could, threw them into a raft and escaped to the island."

"How have you kept from being discovered? Didn't they tell the rangers about you?"

"You mean that we were all here illegally to search for a treasure? Or perhaps that they harbored a runaway from an orphanage in Peru and did unspeakable things to him?"

Peru? Peru? What luck!

Then, he added quickly, "Which they did not, senor; but I could tell the authorities they did." He paused. "No, Senor Hudson. They did not want to stir up a muddy pot."

"Please, Juan. Call me Jim. You saved my life; you can call me anything you want."

"What about you then, Senor Jim? You say you were kidnapped? Why?"

I debated whether I should start right out spilling my guts about the treasure but decided I needed help from somebody, and a young man who had already saved my life once was probably the best bet I could find especially here.

"They killed a man, Juan. Up in the attic of my house in America. Slit his throat from ear to ear." This didn't shock him as much as I'd expected it would. But then, with the troubles he's obviously seen at his tender age, I guess it wouldn't. "They killed him, and they know that I know, and they need to kill me to shut me up." I paused just a moment to let him digest it. "And now, they're going to have to kill you too." I figured that would bond us just a little bit more.

"But why did they kidnap you and bring you here? They could have killed you at sea, dumped your body overboard and been done with it."

Well, here goes: "They kidnapped me to lead them to the treasure of Lima buried somewhere on this island." Didn't faze him much.

"Yes, Senor Jim. I know of the treasure. We read about it in books at the orphanage. Then at night, we would dream and talk about what we would do with the money." He paused and reflected. "We all agreed the first thing we would do is to buy the orphanage and fire the...the...*puta*...the pingona who ran it." My Spanish might be limited, but the intent behind his words was clear enough. After a moment, he came back. "So, you have one of the well-known treasure maps that are supposedly being circulated to unsuspecting *turistas*, have you?"

"No. Juan, I have not. I have the diary belonging to one of the pirates who stole the treasure in the first place."

This raised his eyebrows. "Really, senor?"

"At least I did have it. I think it's still aboard the *Iris*; uh, the yacht anchored in the bay. It damn well better be."

"And how did you come by this diary, Senor Jim?"

"It was in the house I inherited from my great-great-great-grandfather, James Bartholomew Hudson the First."

"He was a pirate?"

"That, he was, Juan. That, he was."

I then proceeded to fill him in on everything that had happened, since I learned of my inheritance. Well, almost everything. I still wasn't ready to divulge my conversations with an ancestor who's been dead for over half a century. That meant I didn't tell him that my main mission was to recover the cross Grandfather had told me about and return it to a church that probably wasn't even standing anymore, so that Grandfather's soul might finally rest in peace. In the end, we agreed that Juan and I would be partners and split whatever we found, minus expenses. With the cot completed and the supper dishes washed, we retired for the night.

I never could quite understand the phrase, "morning comes early." When is it supposed to come? Dawn arrives when the sunlight makes it no longer night. It happens on a definite set schedule, according to one's place on the globe and the time of year. It can't vary itself. If it did, we'd all be in deep kimchi because then we could no longer order our lives according to a clock, and it would drive us all stark raving mad, trying to find out what time it was. Huh. Oh well. At any rate, when that important event did occur, I opened my baby blue eye and my baby green eye to find Juan already up.

"Mornin', Juan," I mumbled, as I rolled off my cot and attempted to put all my dislocated joints back into place.

"Good morning, Senor Jim," he replied. "Fine day to look for treasure. No?"

"Any day's a good day for that, Juan." I chuckled.

After a hearty breakfast of fruit, we found a spot to bury all our garbage, so as not to attract critters...or rangers. Over the months he'd been here, Juan became adept at finding new spots to dig up, where garbage could be buried and the spot camouflaged.

"All right, Senor Jim. Where do we go from here?" he asked.

"Beats he hell out of me, Juan. I don't even know where we are. Before we can find where to go to, we need to know where we're starting from." He chuckled.

Finding a spot of sand by the waterfall pool, I traced as close an outline as I could of the island, then pointed out each landmark.

"Over here on the north side is Chatham Bay. Wafer Bay is here on the northwest side. Down here on the southeast tip is Dampier Head—sometimes called Manta Corner. Now, if you go in a straight line about ten degrees northwest from Dampier Point, about halfway, you'll find Mount Yglesias. That's the highest point on the island. You know where I mean, Juan?"

"Si. I've seen these places many times, but I did not know their names."

I pointed the stick on Mount Yglesias. "This is where I think we should start. That way, we can see most of the island."

"Si. But if we do find the treasure, how will we get it off the island without being detected? We have no boat."

I was about to tell him we may not need a boat because we may be only transporting one cross to Peru, when my words and my arms and my heart turned to ice upon hearing:

"Well now, I think we may be able to help you with that," came the soul-chilling voice of Big Nose behind us. Juan and I wheeled around. Big Nose and Kringle stood twenty or so feet away, both holding guns. Iris was between them and looked more like a prisoner than an accomplice. Her face was symmetrical. The punch to the left side she asked me to give her while we were on the yacht obviously didn't work, since she wore a nearly identical one on the right side, given I was sure by Big Nose out of pure, ill-tempered meanness. She looked at me, fear and degradation in her swollen eyes. It was then I resolved that somewhere down the road and by any means available, I would put a stop to his abuse. I'm a peace-loving man and certainly not a fighter, so I am required by the laws of survival to be devious and ruthless. I swore then and there, it would happen.

With the impetuousness of youth still flowing freely in his blood, Juan made the beginnings of a move toward his crude but efficient bow and arrow, which was leaning against a nearby rock. My arm flew out to stop him, just as Big Nose pulled the trigger, the bullet careening off the top of the rock.

"No!" I yelled to Juan, then turned my attention to Big Nose. "Look," I continued in a sincerely threatening voice—something very foreign to me. "You harm one hair on his head…" I stopped and looked at Iris. "…or hers, and I'll see to it you never ever find that treasure. And you know I'm the only one who can."

Kringle sneered. "We still got the diary."

"You really are as dumb as you look, aren't you?" I paused. "You think I'd still be alive right now if you knew how to find the clues in it? Nope. You need me. This island isn't that big, but it's got a billion hiding places, and you don't have time to look for all of 'em. Better men than you have looked for hundreds of years and haven't found it. But then, they didn't have the diary…or the knowledge to use it."

Kringle began to speak, but Big Nose cut him off. "Shut up, Chris." He turned to me. "Look, Hudson, like I said before, all we want is a piece of the pie. There's plenty enough there for all of us… and then some. We don't wanna hurt you or anybody else." At that point, I almost interjected Jasper's name into the conversation, but thought better of it. Good move. He continued. "What say we go back to our original agreement, find the treasure, split it up and all be on our separate merry ways…a lot richer?"

I knew he was lying through his crooked teeth, but we needed to buy some more time. "That's the first sensible thing I've heard all day," I lied right back at him. "But how do I know you'll keep your word?"

"How do I know you really can find the treasure?"

"Guess that makes us even," I answered. "I may not be able to find it. But you sure as hell won't be able to without me."

"Bargain, then?"

"Bargain." We both lied. But sometimes, you've just got to dance with the devil in the pale moonlight.

"All right, then," he said. "Let's get started."

With that, we began preparing for a long day in a sweltering jungle. Juan started again to retrieve his bow and arrows, but Kringle stood in his way and looked at me.

"Uh-uh," he said. "Better tell Robin Hood here to leave his toys at home. We got guns; that's enough." Juan looked at me. I nodded.

"He ha-bella Englee?" Kringle asked me with another one of his patented sneers. Juan looked him straight in the eyes.

"Better than you, butt-munch," he sneered back. Juan was either blowing smoke at me with his strong Latino accent, or he had mustered every muscle in face, body and brain to sound like he'd just stepped off the E Subway in New York. I suspect the latter, since that pattern was not oft repeated. Kringle laughed a bit; not a happy laugh, a belittling laugh, something completely antithetical to his earlier and obviously phony demeanor.

First, we gathered up what tools we thought we'd need and could carry: a shovel, a pry bar, a pick, about one hundred feet of nylon rope, and all the flashlights and lanterns we could carry from Juan's stash. Filling all the water jugs we could find and stuffing as much fruit as we could into a variety of bags Juan had found lying about on the island and washed out, we set off, with Juan in the lead, me second, Kringle watching us with his gun always handy, Big Nose next, and Iris bringing up our most comely derriere.

Now, it may have just been my imagination, but I could have sworn—or affirmed—that Juan was taking us up Mount MoFo—as we would later christen it—utilizing the most difficult paths he could find. That most affectionate designation was derived in honor of my experience at Fort Irwin, California. It refers to the hill without end. Even on the march back, somehow, they managed to find a way uphill. Never could quite figure that out, but they did it. Having been in a rear-echelon public affairs company, we were out of shape and out of our elements with the infantry, and it pretty well kicked our butts. I wondered if Juan, being the youngest, most agile and in the best physical condition of us all, were deliberately trying to tire us out, so he might make good an escape at the earliest opportunity. I sensed that Big Nose was thinking this also. Periodically, we had to stop and wait for Iris and Big Nose to catch up.

"Hey," he told me, "tell your mountain goat there to ease up a little. We got a woman back here that can't keep up." I nodded compliance, although I suspected he was talking as much about himself, as Iris. After an hour or six, seemingly, we stopped to rest. Those who felt so compelled were allowed to go a few yards into the bushes and relieve themselves. Juan and I, of course, were accompanied by Kringle and his gun. While Juan, under Kringle's watchful eye, and Big Nose were doing their respective duties, I had the opportunity to talk briefly with Iris. I looked at her still-swollen face.

"I'm going to kill him for that," I said. She smiled slightly. "I am," I assured her. I really couldn't believe those words were coming out of my mouth. I, whose pugilistic prowess was pummeled to pieces at the age of ten, never again to be revived. I, whose wit and silver tongue had gotten him out of many matches of strength and agility, with bruisers the size of linebackers. This believer in all things diplomatic was going to beat Big Nose bat crazy, having to go through Kringle and both their guns to do it. Well, my intentions were honorable anyway.

"How'd you get away from the rangers?" I asked, changing the subject.

"They let us go," she replied.

"Say what?"

"Ya. Scott fed them a line of bull about him and me being scientists—bird watchers and such—here to survey wildlife. Chris was our protection against wild boars. He showed them his badge. That's why they heard a shot. He scared off a big one."

"And they bought it?"

"Guess so."

"What about passports and visas?"

"Oh, we told the rangers we left them on the boat for safekeeping. Didn't want to take a chance on losing them in the jungle."

"And they believed that too?" I was incredulous.

"Ya. Pretty dumb, huh?"

I didn't get a chance to answer before Kringle and Juan returned with Big Nose close behind. That having ended our little chat, we resumed our trek up Mount MoFo. We reached the top about 3:00 PM that afternoon. I hadn't told Juan, but Mount Yglesias was part of a riddle I'd found in the diary. It said, "From the crow's nest north, green gives way to blue and gold." Now, the crow's nest, being the highest occupied spot on a ship, could only mean the highest point on the island. That would be Mount Yglesias. Next, we needed to look northward. Unfortunately, escaping the boat did not afford me the opportunity to stock up on survival supplies, and I had no compass. That very necessary implement had also escaped my pursuers' attention. Our last hope was dashed, when Juan admitted that one of the few things he'd not run across, during his sojourn in this inverse utopia, was a compass. Well, we'd just have to guess.

Thinking back to the charts and maps I'd seen of Cocos, it appeared as if the island ran something over forty-five degrees northeast to southwest. Mount Yglesias, only seeming to be as high as Everest when climbing it, was not bare rock at the top. Indeed, it was difficult to determine which direction was which from the ground. By a small clearing (they're all small on Cocos), I found the highest tree I could, laid down my pack and began climbing. Now, kids love to climb everything, especially trees and mountains, with little or no thought of getting back down; a fact that can be verified by nearly any fire department in the world. Adulthood, however, seems to reverse this trend and retard any possibility of adventure overpowering our common sense. As before, my inner child won out over my big-boy sensibility; and I pushed, pulled and swung my appendages like a child possessed. But by the time I'd reached the highest branch I considered safe enough to utilize, my adult body told me my boy's mind had lied to me.

I first looked back down at my insect-sized hiking companions—or so they appeared to my befuddled mind. Whoa! What foolishness had I done now? For a moment, I pondered which branches I would try to use in my careful descent back to the relative safety of two killers who wanted me dead. Oh well. Having expended a considerable amount of my waning energy to get there, I figured I'd better at least get done what I'd climbed up there to do. I looked around.

From my crow's nest, I could see the island stretching northeast and disappearing into a cloud cover. To my left, I could see the cliffs that fell into the ocean at the southwest end. Mentally, I reckoned the northeast end to be at my right hand about seventy degrees. That meant I was facing approximately 290 degrees northwest. Before my arithmetically deprived mind could rebel at this information overload, I spotted a small point sticking out into the blue, where the ocean met the sky. That must be the landmark grandfather was talking about in his diary. My mind raced over the landmarks printed on the maps I had perused. That would be Cabo Barreto or "Baretto Point." As I recalled, that wasn't too far from Wafer Bay, wherein the rangers had their headquarters. That was both good and bad. Good, because it might be a sanctuary we—being Juan, Iris, and me—could utilize to escape from Big Nose and Kringle. Bad, because we'd probably end up spending a year in a Costa Rican prison for illegal entry. Guess a year in jail would be better than eternity in…well, wherever it is we go, if anywhere. Before climbing back down, I looked over toward the opposite side of the island to see if I could identify the sloop, *Iris*, which lay just on the other side of Muela Island. Yup.

I could just make out her mast, sails furled, as she bobbed up and down with the waves. Satisfied I knew our next move, I made my way back down. Juan was still under the constant watchful eye of Kringle and his gun.

"Well?" Big Nose asked.

"Well, what?" I asked back, needling him.

"Don't play games with me, Hudson," he warned.

There's a look that comes in someone's eyes when they're ready to snap. Something that says they have passed the point of reason, and they no longer care about anything. I decided I'd better back off a little.

"The diary talks about facing northward from the crow's nest," I began explaining. "I figure that meant the highest point on the island. That's where we are."

"And?" he menaced.

"And where the green gives way to blue, that's where to find the treasure," I answered, half hoping I was wrong, but also afraid I would be. Big Nose seemed to be getting more desperate and out of control by the minute. I continued. "There's a point due north of here, Barreto Point. I'm guessing that's what he meant by the green of the jungle meeting the blue of the sky or perhaps the sea. Either way, it's clearly the right area.

"What then?"

"Then we climb down to the beach and keep green to green and blue to blue for twenty paces. There should be a boulder in front of a cave entrance. That should be the entrance to where the treasure is hidden."

Kringle piped in, "Green to green and blue to blue? What the hell does that mean?"

"It means," I said, looking at them both, "that I know, and you don't; and I intend to keep it that way until such time as I think I can trust you."

Big Nose tried to put on a conciliatory tone. "Hey, look. We're partners. We're in this together. We have a deal, and I intend to keep my part of the bargain. But we've been working on this for so many years. You can't blame me for getting a little annoyed now and then, can you?"

"Well," I said, knowing he lied, "I've been beaten up and kidnapped, so I guess you couldn't blame me for getting a little suspicious now and then, can you?"

There were a few seconds of tense silence before Big Nose spoke. "Come on. Let's get going."

By the time we reached the tip of Barreto Point, it was nearing dusk. The point was a rock that jutted out into the ocean. The drop was nearly vertical, although on the northeast side, there appeared to be something that could be called a path down about thirty feet. Then it was nearly sheer cliff all the way to another plateau from which one could maneuver down to the beach...such as it was. The beach looked to be no deeper than about twenty to thirty feet. Probably covered at high tide. In a stroke of rare intelligence, Big Nose decided we should spend the night on top rather than risk trying to maneuver down the cliff in poor light.

After a sparse supper of fruit and water, Juan and I were handcuffed to each other and kept under guard. Kringle, Big Nose, and Iris would take turns watching us while the other two slept. I thought it a good sign that Big Nose trusted her enough to guard us. Juan thought we might be able to escape during Iris's watch, but I knew Big Nose would certainly kill her if he thought she screwed up again. Besides, we'd really be hamstrung, trying to run from them while handcuffed together. No. I thought it better we wait for a more opportune time. So, under a huge moon, we settled down for the night.

That opportunity presented itself the next day, although not exactly as I had hoped. Big Nose was anxious to start down the cliff right after sunrise. The first path was doable as was the bottom thirty feet. But the space between needed the rope, which we could only utilize one at a time. Kringle stayed on top to guard us, while Big Nose went first. Next, Juan and Iris, then me. When Kringle saw that Big Nose was guarding us well, he joined us. I looked out to sea, hoping to spot one of the rangers' patrol boats. No luck.

As I was studying Grandfather's diary, it took me a while to understand that when he said "green" and "blue," he was talking not only about the sky, the sea, and the jungle, he was talking about his own eyes…one blue and one green, just like mine. The book said, "When blue meets blue, the direction is true." Hence, if I turned to the right, my blue left eye would meet the blue ocean. OK, I did just that. Turning right, I counted off twenty paces—which nearly ran me out of what little beach there was in that direction. Then, on another one of the pages Grandfather made me memorize, it said, "Now green meets green, where the entrance is seen." Turning toward my right eye, I saw…nothing…nota…zilch…nichts. I stared for a moment, as if my powers of telekinesis could part the rock like Moses parting the Red Sea. Going over to the sheer, solid rock cliff, I began probing little fissures here and there. Nothing. Panic was about to take up residence in me…indeed, in everyone.

"What the hell's goin' on, Hudson?" Big Nose screamed. "I thought you knew where you were going? I don't see any damn caves here! What are you tryin' to pull on me, Hudson?" He grabbed me by the shirt and came nose to nose. "Find it, Hudson!" Out of the corner of my eye, I could see Juan coming to my assistance, but Kringle laid him out with one hand.

Iris rushed in between us. "Stop it! Stop it, Scott!"

Without hardly taking his eyes off me, Big Nose threw a right hook I thought was intended for me but passed right by my nose and landed on Iris's jaw. Down she went. Now, I've heard it said that people who do indeed crack at some point remember very little, if anything, of their actions following the point when their mind splits from their senses. I found that to be mostly true. I vaguely remember my first punch to the same nose I'd hit by accident what now seemed like a decade earlier, followed by a series of them, accompanied by a string of words that I wasn't even sure were words. The next thing I remember was sitting on top of him, trying to make good on my promise to Iris. So, if I was whuppin' the tar out of Big Nose, why did *my* lights go out?

Of course, I woke up with the answer in the form of Kringle, grinning over me. "Hey, that wasn't bad, Hudson. Where'd you learn to punch like that? You'da killed him if I hadn't used Big Bertha here." He waved a blackjack back and forth, like a macho man waving his manhood. How appropriate, I thought.

"Two-time university pugilist champion," I lied. Looking around, I saw Big Nose nursing his welts on one side, while Iris was tending to Juan on the other.

"So, what went wrong, Hudson? How come there's no cave entrance and no treasure?"

"I don't know," I answered. "I followed the directions I remembered from the diary. I'm sure I did. I don't know. I'll have to think back over it and see if I missed something."

Kringle stopped grinning. "Well, don't take too long. Even my patience has its limits." He extended his hand to help me up. One of the rules I'd heard on television when I was growing up was never antagonize the guy with the gun. So, I thanked him and pulled myself up.

"Be a lot easier, if I had the book to look at," I said.

"Well, you know," he replied, "we all kind of left that boat in a hurry. There's a lot of things we didn't bring…including a radio and a compass. Just do the best you can."

Sounded to me like he was trying to play both good cop and bad cop at the same time. Wanting to avoid Big Nose for a while, I sat over by Iris and Juan who was himself just recovering. Iris looked at me with the kind of hero-worship eyes I'd never seen before. I hoped she wouldn't put another lip-lock on me…at least, not right then. I'd had enough scuffling for one day.

Juan got a wry smile on his face. "Looks like we got ourselves into kind of a…" He fought for words. "…how you say? Kind of a cucumber, eh, senor?"

I chuckled. I don't know why. Didn't have a lot to chuckle about. Well, maybe that was it. There wasn't much to chuckle about, so I glommed on to anything I could. "Pickle, Juan. The word is pickle."

"Si. But they are made from cucumbers…no?"

Iris cut in. "Jimmy? Who the hell is Pete Wasnewski?"

"Who?"

"Pete Wasnewski. That's the name you were saying every time you took a swing at Scott."

I really laughed then. All those years of pent-up aggression toward the eleven-year-old bully that beat me up in grade school came pouring out onto Big Nose's face. Well, I couldn't have picked a better target.

"Oh. Nobody, really. Just a kid I knew in school. A very long time ago."

"Senor Jim," Juan asked, "do you have any idea why you could not find the entrance? Was the book wrong?" That got me back on our current task.

"I don't know, Juan. I memorized those pages word for word. I don't know what went wrong. The directions said that when blue meets blue, the direction is true. Now, Grandfather Hudson had weird eyes, just as I do; one blue and one green. I figured that's what he meant by blue meeting blue. When I turned right, my blue eye was on the same side as the blue ocean. When I stopped at the twenty paces, it said, where green meets green, the entrance is seen."

"But there was no entrance, senor."

"I am painfully aware of that fact, Juan," I answered, rubbing my poor jaw.

"Ya. Me too," Iris chimed in.

"But I can't understand," I continued. "His were the same as mine. Green to green and blue to blue. I looked at his painting, hanging in the office of my house. His eyes matched mine perfectly. Just like looking in a mirror. I don't get it."

Juan took me to task. "Senor, what you see in a mirror is you. It is not real, merely the opposite reflection of the real you."

"True."

"When you look into someone else's eyes, that is not an opposite reflection of you. That is another human being. Your left eye is his right, and your right is his left."

They say that realizations sometimes come as flashes and sometimes as lights that start small and burn brighter. There is yet another way we become informed; a fireball drops out of the sky right on top of us, blazing the word "STUPID" behind it in huge burning letters nobody could miss. As he spoke, that fireball slammed right into my face, turning it a bright, bright Dummkopf red that was visible for miles despite my tan from days in the sun.

"AHHHHHHH, CRAP!" My cry echoed across the water, I'm sure being heard on far distant shores by sun revelers who spent the next hour trying to find its source. "What a dummy!" I slapped myself in the head. "Sometimes I think if I had two brains, I'd be twice as stupid." This brought a chuckle from both Iris and Juan as well as the interest of Big Nose and Kringle.

"What's the matter, Hudson?" Kringle asked. "You get it figured out?"

"No, Juan did. Come on," I said, getting up with determination. "Let's go find us a treasure."

Now, why I, all of a sudden, got this bravado, "let's-go-win-this-game" attitude, I haven't a clue. The situation hadn't changed a bit. Juan and I were still prisoners of killers who would probably practice their craft after we found the treasure…maybe kill Iris too. We were still on a miserably hot, bug-infested piece of rock in the Pacific Ocean, nearly out of food, beaten up and sore to the bone. But somehow, the thrill of finding what we'd worked so hard for made all that practically a non-issue. Humans sure are funny.

Going back to my original starting point, I turned left and marched off twenty paces. Turning left again, my entourage and I scoured the face of the cliff for any sign of an entrance.

"There!" cried Kringle. "Over there, by that boulder!"

We all rushed over to a boulder that was nestled neatly into a hole about seven feet high and five feet wide with driftwood piled all around it. Like madmen, we all grabbed driftwood and flung it every which way. Now the boulder. It was flat on the bottom, so it wouldn't roll. Kringle took the pry bar, shoved the tip in between the boulder and the cliff, and began grunting. Juan grabbed the shovel and Big Nose the pick, while Iris and I pulled with our hands.

"On three," Kringle grunted. "One…two…threeeeeee!" It budged just a couple of inches. The rock would not give up its charge easily. "Again! One…two… threeeeee!" Couple more inches. "Again! One…two…threeeee!" This time, it slid a foot. Soon, it was too wide to fit the bar into the slot effectively. Kringle put his back against the cliff with his feet on the rock and shoved.

"Watch out!" I cried, as the boulder began to tumble in Juan's direction. There it was again. In an unexplainable action that went completely against his persona, Big Nose leaped in front of the boulder and pulled Juan to safety. Why? I was sure he was going to kill us anyway. Why not let the boulder do his dirty work? I'm guessing Big Nose was probably asking himself that same question. Human nature sure is funny.

"Thank you, senor," Juan said humbly. Big Nose said nothing, indicating he had realized his mistake.

Now the big moment. I really should have had the honor of entering first, but circumstance being what they were, Big Nose told Kringle to go first with me, Iris, and Juan behind him; Big Nose would bring up the rear, gun in hand. Kringle took the only working flashlight and cautiously stepped in. Juan and I each lit a lamp and followed.

"Careful," I cautioned Kringle. "These places are known to have booby traps." Perhaps I was a victim of our natural tendency to care for others also, just like Big Nose. Had Kringle been incapacitated or even killed by some trap intended to thwart treasure robbers like us, that would have only left Big Nose to worry about…and his gun, of course. But I didn't have that in me either.

The entrance tunnel seemed only twenty feet or so long, slanting uphill. As we emerged into a large cavern that appeared about forty feet in diameter, I could hear water trickling somewhere. Kringle panned his flashlight around, while Juan and I held our lanterns as high as we could. There it was! Just as Grandfather had said. About six feet off the floor on the rock wall was chiseled a crude cross. That meant…that meant I really had seen and talked with my long-dead ancestor. I hadn't been hallucinating. It's difficult to describe my feelings upon this discovery, difficult indeed. I guess I would liken it to the vindication felt by one who believes he had been abducted by aliens and then finds out they are real. I knew I had to conceal my exuberance from the others and did so with great effort. Somehow, I had to recover the cross I knew was buried at the foot of that wall without Big Nose and Kringle knowing. How that would be accomplished was beyond my poor power to add or detract…to paraphrase Lincoln.

On the floor, we could see footprints and skid marks as if heavy things had been dragged into the cave…or out of it. There was only one other passage leading from the main room; I followed it for another twenty feet or so. It ended by a stream that during this dry season had dwindled down to not much more than a trickle. A breeze from the outside nearly blew my lantern out. I heard Big Nose taking my name in vain again.

"Hudson! Hudson! Get in here."

Returning to the main chamber, I found everybody crowded around the only evidence of any treasure that may have been there at one time. It was a chest about two feet long, eighteen inches deep and twelve inches high. Not a lot of treasure there.

"What the hell is this, Hudson?" Big Nose demanded. "One lousy, stinking box? That's what we came two thousand miles for? One box?"

"Well, I didn't put the damn thing there!" I countered. "Don't get on your high horse with me!"

Kringle chimed in. "Quit your belly achin'. Let's see what we got here." He stooped down and picked it up. Wrong move. As soon as he did, out of the ground, popped a skull and crossbones crudely drawn on a board that was attached to a fulcrum. That skull was indeed laughing hysterically. Whoever said pirates didn't have a sense of humor? As we heard rumbling above us and pieces of the ceiling began falling in, one thought raced through our collective mind: BOOBY TRAP!

Big Nose drew his gun and began scrambling backwards toward the entrance, Kringle going first, carrying the box under one arm and Iris under the other. "Sorry, boys," Big Nose said. "Can't let you get out of here. Too much at stake." With that, he began firing as he backed out the entrance, one of his bullets grazing Juan in the arm, just before the entrance completely collapsed…with us inside. I grabbed Juan and dove for the relative safety of the stream.

When the dust settled, as the saying goes, we were nearly in pitch-black. Nearly? That meant there was another exit somewhere. Juan struck a lighter. In the flicker, I could see that one of our old railroad lanterns was still intact. Grabbing it, I held the glass up, while Juan lit the wick, bathing what was left of the cavern in an eerie glow. The entrance was completely blocked. It would take weeks to dig it out by hand, since our shovel and pick had been left outside. That meant we had to follow the stream either to its entrance or exit. The alternative was to starve to death while trying to dig out the cavern entrance. I turned to check Juan's arm.

"You all right?" I asked.

"Si. I am fine, Senor Jim. Only nicked. He was a terrible shot anyway." Juan grinned. Good to keep a sense of humor in tight spots like this.

"Well," I said, "we're going to have to follow this stream to see if we can squeeze through wherever it comes in or goes out." Juan agreed. "But," I continued, "first things first." I picked up the lantern and crawled over to the wall on which the cross was carved. At the bottom, straight underneath it, I began scraping away the dirt. About six inches down, my hand caught a canvass bag that was mostly rotted away. Like a man possessed by the greed of every pirate on board the *Mary Deare*, my hands flew dirt in every direction until one of them wrapped around an object that was either the handle of a dagger or a cross. What I pulled out was the latter. It seemed less ornate than I had imagined it to be. Certainly, it was made of gold and had three or four jewels imbedded in it; but it fell far short of my sweet imagination. Still, it was *the* cross; the one that would finally set poor Grandfather's soul free from the purgatory he has occupied for over fifty years. I had, thus far, kept my promise to him. I rather chuckled to myself. Now, all that remained was to find a way out from being buried alive and make our way to a two-hundred-year-old church that probably isn't even standing anymore, some eleven hundred nautical miles away…without a boat. As one comedian has said, a piece of milk.

It wasn't as difficult to locate the stream's outlet as I thought it might be. There was a narrowing of the tunnel down to about eighteen inches or so and an overhang that dropped it down even more. Juan and I took turns chiseling away at that overhang with rocks from the cave-in and finally broke enough off for us to squeeze through. The outlet was about ten feet off the ground, so we had to slide out feetfirst on our bellies. Even so, it was a bit of a shock to our legs, especially my near-middle-aged ones.

We rested for a bit behind some driftwood and bushes, not knowing where Big Nose, Kringle, and Iris might have gone. Once we decided they were probably not around, we began the trek back up the cliff. Big Nose must have assumed we were dead because they didn't bother retrieving the rope we had used to get down the cliff. So far, so good. At the top of Mount MoFo, I climbed the same tree to see if the *Iris* were still anchored. Nope. Gone. Good. Now, all I had to do was figure out how to get to Lima with Grandfather's cross. It was near dark when Juan and I reached the cave behind the waterfall. Both dog tired, we all but fell onto our cots and passed out like drunks.

# CHAPTER TEN

My encounter with Grandfather that night was not real; I know it wasn't. It was a dream. But what a dream! He and I were shipmates who had been pressed into service aboard a pirate ship that was in a huge battle with a Spanish galleon. We had boarded the galleon but did our best not to hurt anybody. Hey. It was a dream...OK? It was my dream, and I don't like violence in my dreams. Two damsels—one the ship's cook who looked like... like a cook, and the other a lovely Contessa who bore a remarkable resemblance to Iris—were about to be set upon by the brigands in our crew. With cutlasses swinging, Grandfather and I jumped in to save them, vanquishing all the brigands. It was a dream; it didn't have to make sense. Just as we were about to receive our kisses of undying gratitude, I heard the unmistakable sound of a pistol cocking right next to my head.

No. I mean I *really* heard a pistol cocking next to my head. My eyes flew open to find the bore of a Model 1911A1, .45 caliber Remington staring right back at me, not four inches from my face. I was really getting tired of staring down the business end of a bang stick. Attached to this government surplus death machine was the hand of what had to be the scariest-looking human alive...well, I think it was human. I guessed his age to be somewhere between fifty and five hundred years old, possibly closer to the latter. Black hair that gnarled halfway down to his shoulders and really needed an oil change, crowned a face with thin, unshaven cheeks and a flat nose that had probably been made so by numerous fists. His name was, as I later learned, Ignacio, but I decided to call him Snaggletooth. As he spoke, I was sure the four teeth he had left would soon be three.

"Buenos dias, senor." He grinned. "¿Tiene un lindo sueño?"

I looked over at Juan who was being guarded by a linebacker… well, a guy that probably could play that position on any NFL team. From my perspective, he appeared about eighteen feet high and seven feet wide. He was African in ancestry with close-cropped hair, a broad face and a smile to match. His voice was deep and resonating…and French.

Juan anticipated my inquiry. "He wants to know if you had a pleasant dream, Senor Jim."

"Tell him, yes. Until I woke up. Now, it's a nightmare," I answered. Juan translated, and Snaggletooth laughed along with Linebacker and the other three real-life brigands who were holding Juan, me, Wishy, Big Nose, Kringle, and Iris captive. I did a double take on my four previous captors who were also being held at gunpoint. Wishy, Big Nose, and Kringle all looked like they'd just played four quarters of football against the Green Bay Packers…without the benefit of helmets or pads. Hard telling with Iris. She'd looked like that before. Wishy was shaking like a dog-pooping tacks. Two of them jerked me off the cot and threw me down next to him, while Linebacker and two others conferred in quiet Spanish.

"What the…? Where'd you guys come from?"

"They tricked us," Wishy said in a whisper, calming down a bit. "They pretended their boat was on fire, and when we stopped to help them, they boarded us." He paused to see if any of the brigands were listening, then continued. "They were going to kill us all…well, except for Iris. When they found the little box full of gold coins, we were able to convince them that you knew where the rest of the treasure was." He paused again. "We took them back to the treasure cave to help dig you out, when we found your footprints below the little waterfall. We figured you'd make your way back here." He paused and began to tremble again. "We knew we were just buying time, and if you'd been dead in the cave, our time would have run out. This buys us a little more time, that's all." The Hispanic brigand behind him cut Wishy off with a slap to the back of the head.

"¡Silencio!"

I looked back at Juan. "What do they want?"

Linebacker answered with an unmistakable French accent. "The remainder of the treasure, monsieur."

"What treasure?" I asked. "We didn't find any treasure."

"Ah, mon ami," Linebacker said. "Please do not play games with us. That would be very bad. We found the small container of coins your friends had on their boat. It required some…shall we say, persuasion, but they finally told us all about your 'journal intime—your diary—and the treasure to which it leads."

I couldn't let them find the cross. I couldn't. "I'm telling you, there… is… no… treasure!"

Linebacker barked an order in Spanish, and two of the brigands began tearing the place (such as it was) apart. The brigands appeared to be in their thirties or forties. One was Caucasian with a butch cut, high cheekbones and beady eyes that seemed devoid of life. The other was possibly Filipino, average build and sported the most intricate tattoos I'd ever seen from head to toe. I guessed they were tribal tattoos. I'd read of them and seen pictures, but they paled in comparison to the real thing. An absolute walking, talking and now house-wrecking work of art. So, here we had it. Two Hispanics, a black Frenchman, one Caucasian, and a Filipino. The pirate's answer to the United Nations. Well, I'd always read that the pirates of old were more inclusive than some so-called democratic nations. Guess so.

It was only a matter of time until they found the cross stuffed into one of the backpacks. As Tattoo pulled it out, eighteen eyes grew huge, bulging nearly out of their sockets. Well, make that sixteen, for sure. It was hard to tell with Butch Cut. There was a virtual Babylon of exclamations.

"¡Caray!" "Hot damn!" "*Ca alors!*" "Wow!" "*Unglaublich!*" I reasoned that probably meant Butch Cut was German. Given his appearance, I imagined him in a leather trench coat, a broad-brimmed fedora and sporting an SS pin.

"Well, Monsieur Hudson," Linebacker said, "it seems you have indeed been playing silly games with us. I think you would be wise to dire *la vérité*…how you say, come clean with us. Otherwise, very bad things could happen to you and your friends." He paused to let it sink in. "Now, where is the remainder of the treasure, Monsieur Hudson?"

"I keep telling you there *is* no more treasure. What you have is what there is."

"Monsieur, your friends here have said differently."

"They lied. They were there, when we got into the cave. They saw it was not there. Somebody had already gotten to it. They lied."

Linebacker turned his gaze to Iris. "She is very beautiful, Monsieur. No? It would be a shame to kill such a lovely creature." He barked orders in Spanish again. Snaggletooth pulled her up from behind savagely by the hair, wrapping his arm about her, like the depraved brute he was. Butch Cut flicked open a switchblade and began lightly tracing the point around her face and body. Iris was terrified. "Or perhaps," he continued, "I could sell her to some very fine business enterprises I know. She would fetch a good price, monsieur."

"All right!" I shouted. "All right! Just let her go! I'll tell you everything I know about the treasure and help you find it. Please, just let her go." Linebacker nodded, and Snaggletooth pushed a sobbing Iris back down next to Big Nose who all but ignored her when she buried her face in his shoulder to weep. As disgusted as I was with Big Nose, I had other things to occupy my mind at the time; like how was I going to lead these killer animals to a treasure that doesn't exist? And how was I going to get Grandfather's cross away from them and to an ancient church that also may not exist anymore? Wow.

"Look," I said, "what I told you was true. We didn't find the treasure because somebody had already gotten it. But I think I know where they took it many, many years ago."

"And where would that be, where, monsieur?"

"In a church east of Lima, Peru. It's an old church that nobody uses anymore, but it's got a big underground storage area. That's where I think they took it. The location is coded in the diary."

"Yes, monsieur, we have that book. It is very confusing."

"Not to me. I have the key. I can find it."

"And you will, monsieur."

"But let me tell you one thing," I warned. "If you dare to harm one hair on that woman, I will never ever lead you to the treasure… or anything else. I will die first."

"That you may do anyway, monsieur. But I will give you my word that neither I nor my crew will harm her in any way. But let me tell you this in return, monsieur. If you are lying to me, the consequences will be far greater than you could ever imagine…not in your worst nightmare, monsieur." Linebacker paused. "Do we have a deal, monsieur?"

"We do," I assured him. With that, we shook hands and prepared to depart once again. Funny. I knew he would kill us as soon as he'd found the treasure; and he knew I'd rat him out to the authorities at the earliest opportunity. Yet, we shook hands on a bargain we both knew was bogus. The folly of man.

I tried to get Linebacker to let me carry the cross, but he would have none of it; he would carry it himself. I knew he'd be with me the whole way, so that satisfied me. When we got down to the beach on the southwest end of the island, near where the Iris had been anchored, there was not a boat, skiff or raft in sight. Linebacker had us all wait, hidden behind what little vegetation there was, until dark. He recovered a radio from a small alcove in the rock and contacted somebody to come and get us after dark. That was a few hours away, so we figured it would be a good idea to get some sleep. The brigands slept in shifts with two of them watching us at all times. Iris sat down between Juan and me.

"Thank you again, Jimmy," she said. "I owe you more than I can ever repay."

"No thanks necessary, Iris," I answered. "I had to make sure they'd leave you alone."

Her eyes took on that same distant look they'd had on board the boat, when I discovered that Big Nose had used her for a punching bag. "Well, I guess it's a little too late for that, but I love you for trying, Jimmy. That's more than Scott ever did."

I froze. I didn't know what to say, except, "I'm sorry, Iris. I'm so sorry." I put my arm around her shoulders, and she laid her head on my chest. With that, we laid down and tried to sleep. As I lay there, trying to make some sense of the last couple of…weeks? months? decades? Well, as I lay there contemplating the beauty sleeping in my arms, I somehow didn't really care that her husband was fifteen feet away. It just didn't matter anymore, not to me and apparently not to him. I wondered how my life will have changed; were we lucky enough to survive this ordeal? My mind then shifted to the more pressing business at hand: finding the church and still keeping us alive. In a sense, they were mutually exclusive. If I found the church and there was no treasure, Linebacker would surely kill us; if I found the church and there was treasure, which I doubted, they would probably kill us anyway; if I didn't find the church, there would be no chance at all of finding treasure, and he would kill us then too. There was no scenario—except escape or rescue by authorities—that did not end with our being killed. Didn't look good for the home team sports fans.

As I pondered these things, I could see above the undulating treetops a lone gull, as it glided thither and yon, round and round our little campsite, as if to stand sentry against an uncertain future. Was it my friend with the black belt of dirty feathers? Couldn't tell from that distance. I pretended it was. Even with all these weighty worries or perhaps because of them, my eyelids slowly began to take me into that ethereal world of fictional fears and fervid fancies we all enter, when the world we know outside shuts its doors. Being in such close proximity to the epitome of both beauty at her best and the beast at his worst, I will leave the contents of those fears and fancies locked safely away in the cells of my psyche to be visited only as needed or desired…alone.

Activity around me roused me out of my reverie. It was dark, although a huge moon brightened things up, whenever a break in the gathering clouds allowed it. Iris was still asleep. I fought the urge to kiss her forehead. Why? I don't know, perhaps it was because I had never lost my innate shyness with women; and her being a married woman, whose husband was now up and walking around, compounded my problem exponentially. I shook her lightly.

"Iris," I said in a horse whisper. "Iris, wake up. We're going to be pulling out soon."

She yawned and smiled at me. "Well, that wasn't a very nice thing to do."

"What's that?"

"Wake a girl out of a beautiful dream like I was having. That's downright unchivalrous."

I chuckled a bit. "And what was that?"

"Oh, no. You ain't gettin' that out of me; well, at least, not here." She laughed.

"When we get out of this, we'll have to compare."

She laughed again. It was a good laugh, a warm laugh.

"Monsieur Hudson," Linebacker interrupted, "the launch will be here in a few moments. We will take half at a time. The trip out will take about fifteen minutes."

We all took turns behind the little men's room bush with a guard standing by. Big Nose refused to accompany Iris to the little girl's room, so I did, standing between Iris and the guard. When the launch arrived, Iris, Kringle, and Wishy were to be first. I didn't particularly like that arrangement. I didn't think Kringle and Wishy would give her the protection she needed.

"Just a minute," I told Linebacker. "I'll go in place of this one." I gestured to Wishy.

"Monsieur Hudson," he said, "I gave you my word." I said nothing, just stared into Linebacker's eyes, telling him what I thought of his word. He relented. "Very well. You may accompany."

"Did you tell your crew that you gave your word?" I inquired.

"Yes, monsieur, I did. But I will repeat it to them again...just for you." With that, he shouted orders to the boat crew in Spanish. I looked to Juan for interpretation. He nodded. Wishy and I exchanged places, and the crew shoved off.

A few minutes later, I could see the outline of a fishing boat becoming larger. As we drew near, I could see it was an old fishing boat, probably forty-five feet or so. It had a wider beam than the *Iris*. Couldn't see her name in the dark. As we tied up and the crew began helping us aboard, I heard the launch operator say something very emphatically to the crew on deck. Although I didn't know their meaning, several of the words sounded much like the orders

Linebacker had shouted. I felt a little more at ease. As I boarded, I saw what looked like three or four smudge pots—like those used in citrus groves to warm fruit in cold weather—sitting at various locations on deck. That's what they'd used to fool Big Nose into thinking they were in distress. Clever.

There were only two more brigands on board, and they both appeared Hispanic… and they had guns. We were herded down into what had been one of the fish tanks. Although it appeared it had been converted to hold dry cargo—probably drugs or other contraband—it still stunk. There, we were shackled to a cargo tie-down bar that ran the length of the inner hulls between and along the bulkheads. One brigand held a gun on us as the other did the work.

When I heard the lock of the chain close around my leg, a picture flashed through my mind. I felt I was getting just an infinitesimal taste of what the slaves who were captured in Africa and shipped to America might have known, under conditions worse than even animals would need endure. As I said, it was an infinitesimal taste, but it was enough. I fought that feeling with all my mental and physical strength because I could feel the rage welling up inside of me, and I knew that would be counterproductive to my efforts in getting us out of this latest predicament. I decided I needed to defer that rage to a proper time and place.

"What happened to the yacht?" I asked Iris.

Kringle answered, "Probably halfway across the Pacific by now to be sold on the black market."

Wow. No wonder Big Nose was in such a perpetual foul mood. Although not of the Queen Mary stature, it had been at one time, a pricey bathtub toy. But that still didn't excuse his violent conduct with Iris; nothing excuses that. We sat mostly in silence for the next forty-five minutes or so until the remainder of the crew and captives arrived.

When that less-than-auspicious occasion occurred, Big Nose, Juan, and Wishy were chained on the inner hull opposite us. Everyone was sullen, and anyone who said they were not frightened was either a liar or crazy. After the newcomers where secured, we heard the engine fire up. Big Nose perhaps couldn't help displaying to us his seafaring knowledge.

"That's a souped-up four-hundred-thirty horse Merc, eight point two. In a tub like this, she'll cruise about twelve knots—give or take—but it can go a lot faster. For what these guys transport, they need the speed to get where they're going in the dark. Take us roughly four days to get to Lima, give or take; maybe three, if they're in a hurry."

"You know all that from hearing the motor, senor?" Juan asked.

"No. When he stole my boat, he took me down to his engine room to rub my nose in it. It's like two drag racers, where one has to brag why his is better."

"What about fuel?" I asked.

"They got plenty. They don't wanna be stoppin' at no gas stations with a load of drugs or stolen contraband on board."

The next three days were relatively routine...not comfortable, but routine. We were each allowed up on deck for an hour a day under close armed guard. Out of curiosity, each time that occasion arose, I looked around for my seagull friend. I saw gulls, but they were always too far away to tell. Linebacker seemed to be keep his word, and I know of no harassment Iris suffered from him or the crew. Bathroom breaks were always individually and under guard. I was not allowed to accompany Iris as far as the head door, but I felt she was safe...well, as safe as any of us could be in the hands of blood-thirsty modern-day pirates. The food they offered was not fancy—soup, sandwiches and water—but it sustained us.

I must say, this experience was the antidote that cured any lingering boyhood fantasies I may have had about pirates, then or now, being glamorous. I figured it's like other endeavors that the immature young and the immature old fancy as dirty but glamorous...such as war. But when one actually is thrust into the real thing, the glamor dies and the feculence flies. Considering what I'd learned from him, Grandfather was probably one of those immature boys who crossed over into a world he knew nothing about and from which he had not the ability to extricate himself.

On that third day, I lost my innocence. That day will live more than any other in my soul. It will occupy a cell in my psyche that has no windows, for it is an abomination to humanity and deserves no attention, save as a reminder of the depths to which man will stoop, as a slave to greed. We could hear two pirates discussing in Spanish. After they moved out of our earshot, I asked Juan what they'd said. He told us that we would be reaching our destination sometime the next evening; a small island called Isla del Asia, some sixty miles south of Lima, a just off the coast. There, we would transfer to the mainland again and thence to…? That's when the two moved away.

Sometime later—it could have been minutes or hours—time does not measure well under such circumstances; our individual afternoon strolls began. Wishy went first this time. His hands were secured behind him, and he was helped up the ladder. From down in our stinky hold, we could hear Linebacker talking with him in low, quiet tones, too low to understand their content. Wishy began to whimper, then whine, then scream; then a single shot signaled his silence. Iris began to cry. The shock each of us felt travelled effortlessly around us and through us, gaining in strength and electrifying the air. Our solemnity had morphed into mournful fear. Our eyes locked onto each other's in turn, wondering who would be next. Again, some incalculable amount of time passed before we heard the executioners' footsteps again. This time, it was Juan they took.

I screamed obscenities at them, hoping they would get angry enough to take me instead. "No! Come on, you cowardly, scum-sucking bastards! He's just a kid! Take me!"

I was, of course, ignored, as they escorted a trembling fifteen-year-old boy to his doom. We all waited for the single shot…but there was none. As we waited, I looked at Iris. We were all going to die quickly. She would suffer unimaginable indignities before the bullet entered her brain. Perhaps it would have been better if I had let her drown. God forgive me again, but the thought of a mercy killing flashed through my mind. But as such things have before, it quickly dissipated and left my face with a crimson glow of shame.

Again, the executioners' steps were heard. Kringle was next under double guard, considering his size. Again, no shot. One by one, we three remaining were brought on deck. I was the last. As I joined the others, I saw Wishy's body wrapped tightly in a blanket and weighted down, lying on the deck next to the gunwale.

Linebacker addressed us with a smile...a *smile!* "Good afternoon, mes amis. Please forgive our intrusion into your daily...how you say, constitutional. But as you can see, Monsieur Aloysius has had some...difficulty. He violated our sacred rule and refused to cooperate with our simple requests. Therefore, he was required to suffer the consequences. Such a shame too." We were all silent and stone-faced as he continued. "We thought it appropriate that you join us in paying our last respects to this man." Again silence.

Linebacker nodded, and two of his crew picked Wishy up, paused at the edge of the gunwale and, upon confirmation from Linebacker, dropped him into the sea. I noticed that any blood which may have been on the deck had been washed away. Everything looked so neat. It reminded me of the old movies I used to watch, wherein people would get shot and fall down dead without spilling a drop of blood. We all grew up with the impression that killing, whether in the West, on the streets, or in a war, was tidy and uncomplicated. Humans are so delusional. The burial detail then, along with Linebacker and the crew, rendered a salute. Some made the sign of the cross. Linebacker turned back to us. "Now," he said. "Please keep this in mind as we journey together through these next several difficult days. All I require is cooperation. That is the only cardinal rule I have." He paused. "Do you have any questions of me?"

I was tempted to ask if he'd already made his own reservations in hell, but I thought better of it. There being no questions from us stunned and shaken prisoners, we were all taken one by one—with stops at the head, if necessary—back down into our smelly apartment. Once settled, some of us got as comfortable as possible and slept, Iris with her head on my chest.

I didn't think anything could stink as bad as that fish hold; that is, until we reached the proximity of Isla del Asia. As I discovered, Isla del Asia is the most prolific producer of a natural fertilizer called guano—i.e., bird poop. It is mined there, just like iron ore in Minnesota, only iron ore doesn't stink. The island has a number of small inlets and a dock. That's it. Perfect place for bad guys to meet in the middle of the night. Who wants a vacation home on an island covered in a hundred feet of smelly bird poop?

I guessed it to be about midnight, when we transferred from the trawler to three smaller boats and made the trip to the mainland. Again, we ran without lights, the moon being bright. In between the clouds, it brightened up the area enough to see we were heading toward what appeared to be an industrial park full of warehouses. As we sat aboard the speeding boat, I gazed up at the moon. Periodically, I could see flashes of birds whizzing past in silhouette. Night birds? Looked like gulls. Was it two or three in succession or just one zipping back and forth? Couldn't tell. Hmmm. I guessed I'd seen them buzzing around before at night. Didn't pay much attention to them, though.

When we reached the dock, they did something that may have given me a little flash of hope that, in the end, they would not kill us after all. Once on the dock, we were blindfolded and led to a waiting van that had no windows in the back. Why, if they were bent on killing us anyway, would they take such measures to hide our location and route from us? Perhaps another fool's false hope...but a hope nonetheless. Bound and blindfolded, it seemed to take forever to go...wherever. Two guards sat watching us to make sure we wouldn't try any shenanigans.

The skies were just beginning to lighten, when we entered the compound of a somewhat lavish hacienda. We were taken out of the van, and our blindfolds removed. What I could see of it seemed perhaps a hundred feet wide. Paved walkways wound through beautiful palm trees and flower gardens. The length of the compound I could not determine because of the beautiful hacienda in front of us. Its two stories were complete with balconies and a portico.

We were then herded inside and made comfortable—as one can be while still bound—on leather couches in the tastefully decorated parlor. One thing I noticed, both inside and out in this South American Shangri-La, were the number of armed guards of both sexes stationed nearly in every corridor and room as well as on the roof, armed with sniper rifles. The lucrative business of smuggling drugs and other merchandise certainly does come at a price. It made me appreciate that I could live in a nice, if not lavish, house without needing armed guards…that is, if I were ever to see it again.

Presently, Linebacker joined us. "Bonjour, mes amis. Welcome to my humble abode. I hope your stay will be pleasant; brief but pleasant." He received no response, not even a smile. "Again, mes amis, I have but one cardinal rule and that is for you to do exactly as you are told, when you are told." He paused. "Oh, and you will of course have noticed that my associates are everywhere here. They have had strict instructions that any one of you—yes, even you, Monsieur Hudson, are to be shot dead if he or she were to attempt an escape. Please keep that in mind, mes amis." Still no response from any one of us. He continued. "And now, since we have all had such a long, arduous and smelly journey, hot showers, clean clothes and a soft bed await you all." He began to leave but stopped and turned back. "Mister Hudson, when we are all sufficiently rested, I will need to speak to you concerning the route we will be taking this evening."

With that, we were all herded to our accommodations for the day. And quite comfortable they were at that. We were doubled up. I was with Big Nose—an arrangement I thought the antithesis of good planning but decided the less Linebacker knew of us individually, the better. Kringle and Juan were roommates. Iris got a bedroom to herself, something I was glad to see, since I didn't think Big Nose deserved her. I wondered if Linebacker even knew they were married. Couldn't recall any time that might have come out unless it had been when they were first captured.

I had no concept of how good a hot shower could feel. Afterward, we were given night clothes—silky pajamas, no less—and allowed to crash onto our individual queen-sized beds. This guy had apparently taken a liking to A-plus hotels, since his guest rooms reflected their comfort. A well-appointed air-conditioned room in a beautiful South American setting…wow. As I settled in for the night…uh, day, I reasoned that, were it not for the likelihood of ending up dead soon, this would have been a great way to end a vacation.

Big Nose and I had not spoken a word since our arrival. He crawled under his covers and settled in also before he spoke. "You can have her," he said in a matter-of-fact tone.

"What?"

"You can have her," he repeated. "She's been a millstone around my neck anyway. Take her. The sooner, the better."

I said nothing. I guessed this was quite in keeping with Big Nose's persona. She was an object to him, nothing more. That caused me some consternation because it forced me to confront my own feelings. Wow. Did I really want her, or was I just so enamored of her beauty and fun personality (under normal circumstances) that I just thought I did? Wow. Now, I had trouble sleeping. I mentally cursed Big Nose for that, figuring maybe he was just trying to get under my skin, which he did. Eventually—I had no idea when—the exhaustion of the last few days overcame my angst, and I dipped into a sleep so deep I thought Grandfather would have to travel farther into purgatory just to locate me, which he apparently didn't, since we did not meet.

# CHAPTER ELEVEN

I was awakened just after dusk by Butch Cut flipping on the light and calling out, apparently without caring if he woke Big Nose also. "Herr Hudson! Herr Hudson. You will please get dressed and follow me. I will be right outside the door."

With a start, I sat up. Whatever dream I'd been having disappeared quickly in my haste to follow instructions. Reverting back to my glory days in the Army National Guard, I threw on the clothes they had laid out for me, laced up my old deck shoes and bounded out the door, nearly slamming into Butch Cut.

"Hey!" I heard Big Nose yelling from within. I knew just exactly what he wanted, so I reached back in the door and flipped off the light. "Thank you," came the acknowledgement.

As we descended the stairs into the study, I could smell the delicious meal being prepared for us in the kitchen. I'd forgotten how hungry I was. Now, my stomach reminded me constantly. I only hoped it wouldn't be my last.

We entered a beautiful Spanish-style study with rows of books lining the walls. A huge globe sat in the middle of the floor. Stuffed chairs and two love seats centered the room. In a corner stood a huge birdcage occupied by the most beautiful and richly appointed Macaws I had ever had the pleasure of seeing. Linebacker had a map of Peru laid out on a table that was against one of the walls.

"Ah, Monsieur Hudson," he greeted me warmly. "So good of you to join me early. I saw no need to awaken the others just yet. May I offer you something to drink? Coffee, perhaps? Since we've such a long night ahead of us, I would not recommend consuming any alcohol."

"Coffee would be fine. Thank you." Butch Cut went to get it. "Black," I added, as he left.

Linebacker escorted me to the map. "Now, Monsieur Hudson, as to the location of our treasure."

"*Our* treasure?" I thought.

Linebacker continued. "You are the only one who has the key to its location stored in your head. A very valuable head it is, too, monsieur. Everyone is well aware of the Lima treasure, Monsieur Hudson. It is large enough to accommodate all our needs, so there will be no need for us to kill you or your friends. That is, unless you attempt to cross us doubly, monsieur. In which case, the Amazon alligators will feast heartily." He paused to let it sink in, then continued. "If we do find the treasure, monsieur, we will not pig it all. We will give you two things from our collective efforts. We will give you each some of the treasure; certainly not as much as you would have gotten alone, but some. We will also give you your lives, monsieur. Despite the violent business in which I deal, I find it much better to strike a bargain of trust and mutual benefit than to go about killing people…how you say, willy-nilly."

I thought about this a moment. He was either giving me a false sense of security, or he was on the level…well, as much as a thief and killer could be. I figured I'd follow Teddy Roosevelt's sage words about speaking softly, but carrying a big stick, except I didn't have much of a stick to carry.

"What about Wishy?" I asked.

"Ah, yes. Monsieur Aloysius. He had two bad things working against him, monsieur. First, he was a banker. I detest bankers. They lure people into buying things they don't need on credit they shouldn't have. Then, when the poor souls can't pay, the bank takes everything, leaving them with nothing. I have seen it many times, and I deplore it."

"So, that's a reason to kill him?"

"Possibly not. But Monsieur Aloysius also was a rodent, Monsieur Hudson, a rat, if you will. He offered to sacrifice all of you in return for his own life. That to me, Monsieur Hudson, is the lowest form of life there is. So, I determined the world was probably better off without him."

"*You* determined," I thought to myself but wasn't dumb enough to say out loud. "What right do you have to determine who lives or dies?" Then out loud I said, "I guess I can't argue that one."

"So you see, Monsieur Hudson, we can strike a bargain, you and myself."

Being French, I forgave him his bad English and answered, "You mean, I lead you to the treasure. In return for our silence, you give us some of it and let us go."

"Oui, monsieur. You lead me to the treasure. The others may stay here in relative comfort. Then, when we return, we will divide up the proceeds, and you may go free."

I didn't like being separated from the others, strength in numbers and all that, I guess. "All right. It's a deal," I agreed. "But I want the others to go with us. I want us all to be together."

Linebacker thought a moment. "Oui. I agree, monsieur," he said, offering his hand. With that, we shook hands on a deal that was as tenuous as life itself. We leaned over the table to study the large map of Peru that covered the entire tabletop and then some. He continued. "Where shall we begin, monsieur? Where shall we begin our fantastic journey into time and riches beyond our wildest imagination?"

I thought for a moment, going back through the pages Grandfather had made me memorize in order. The first ones got us to the empty cave on Cocos Island. I guessed then that the remaining pages told me how to get to the church, since that would be the next move in my quest to free his immortal soul. One of them said this:

"One hundred leagues, plus twenty-five
Where rainbows consume the earth
That's where straightaway you fly
To be near God and near my worth."

I repeated this to Linebacker. We pondered and puzzled over this for quite some time before we decided to break it down into its parts.

"One hundred leagues, plus twenty-five, monsieur. Sailors haven't used that unit of measure since…forever." He crossed over to a wall of books and picked one out. "Here, Monsieur Hudson. I have a book of conversions." Opening it up, he found what we needed. "One league equals three point four five statute miles, monsieur."

"That's approximately four hundred thirty-one and one quarter miles," I said, doing quick calculations on the edge of the map. From the legend, we measured a string to the approximate length and anchored its base in the heart of Lima, then drew a north and south arc. Wow. That was a lot of territory to explore. Even taking off those areas that were not jungle, left some one thousand miles or so of arc to search, even more when one accounts for the inaccuracy of measurements in Grandfather's day. Butch Cut brought my very-welcome coffee, then stood at his post by the door.

"Well, now that we have an approximate distance, let's work on the other part of the puzzle," I suggested. "Where rainbows consume the earth?" We bounced that back and forth for a long time but came up empty-handed. Then, I remembered Juan was from this area. Linebacker sent Butch Cut to fetch him.

"You wanted to see me, Senor Hudson?" Juan asked, as he entered.

"Yes, Juan," I answered. "We're stuck on a puzzle that has to do with this area, and we're hoping you can help us out."

"I'll do what I can, Senor Hudson."

We filled Juan in on everything we had done and discussed thus far. We ended with the "where the rainbow consumes the earth" part. Juan pondered this a while.

"Well, senor," he began, with a puzzled look. "The only thing I can think of would be the rainbows caused by the mist of a waterfall. Those are the only ones that one sees in one place consistently."

"No. We already thought of that, Juan," I explained. "Couldn't find any waterfalls large enough for that on the map." We were all getting a little bit frustrated, when those beautiful, wonderful macaws in the corner decided to tell us just how ignorant humans can be. They both began to chatter, squeal and whistle. At first, it was annoying. I turned to them and yelled, as if they could understand.

"Shut up! You pair of..." My voice trailed off as I looked at their beautifully colored feathers, a veritable rainbow of colors. My voice started back up again. "You pair of...lovely... beautiful...rainbow-colored *sweethearts*!" I turned to Linebacker and Juan. "That's it! Not rainbows, but colorful birds!"

"But, mon ami," Linebacker said, "there are millions and millions of colorful birds in Peru that nest in a million more places. How can that help?"

"Any of them eat dirt?"

Juan began to grin. "Not eat, senor, but lick." The light began going on in Linebacker's head also. Juan continued. "The macaws, Senor, have a very strange diet that includes seeds and plants that are toxic, not only to humans, but to macaws themselves. To counteract these toxins, macaws find certain grades of clay, usually around some riverbeds, where they lick the clay. This certain type of clay, senor, contains antitoxins that neutralize the poison in the bird's body. Macaws are the rainbows that consume the earth."

"But there has to be hundreds, maybe thousands of these clay licks in Peru, monsieur," Linebacker said. "How do we find the right one?"

"Yes," I answered, "but how many would be on a four hundred thirty-two mile arc east of Lima?"

I guess it made sense to Linebacker because he went immediately back to the map and began looking at points of interest. One caught his eye southeast of Lima. It said, *Parque Nacional del Manu*. "Manu National Park, mes amis. I suddenly remembered reading something about there being large flocks of macaws that like the clay banks there. That could be the location." Going over to a shelf crammed with books, he withdrew a large travel book and thumbed through it until he found what he wanted. His face brightened, as he offered it to us for inspection. "See, this must be what he was talking about." There was a story about the macaw clay licks and a map that seemed to coordinate perfectly with the big map on the table. There is an earthen airstrip about sixty or seventy kilometers from there by the biological station. The officials there let us use it quite often. It can accommodate our aircraft. We have used it many times." I didn't dare ask him, for what? But I could probably guess.

"Yes. So it appears," I said. "It gets us closer for sure."

"And after that, monsieur?" Linebacker asked.

"After that," I said, tapping my head, "it's all in here." Linebacker smiled and nodded at my barefaced lie. I had no idea where we were headed after that. Not a clue. At that point, the cook, a stocky, hard-looking lady of about fifty or so announced that dinner would be on in a few minutes. Linebacker had Butch Cut go wake the others to meet us in the dining room.

Since none of us had eaten a real meal in weeks, we devoured this fine feast of braised duck, vegetables, sweet potatoes, a kind of plum pudding dessert, and a very fine wine. I will ashamedly admit that I had forgotten or perhaps purposely ignored the fact that this sustenance came sautéed in blood and seasoned with sorrow. But then, I guessed that going on a hunger strike with this obviously refined animal would serve no good purpose at all.

At the end of the meal, he addressed us. "Atención, s'il vous plait," he said in a rare mix of Spanish and French. "My honored guests, I hope you have enjoyed your meal. We employ here the finest chef south of Lima." Well, I guess he let our location slip just a little bit. Now, we would know which direction to run, were we to escape, which was a very remote possibility. He continued. "Monsieur Hudson and I, with the assistance of Juan here, believe we have narrowed down the location of the church we seek...and the treasure that is buried beneath it." There was no joy in Mudville over this revelation. Any enthusiasm that might have been felt was quickly quelled by the knowledge that our own lives here were just as tenuous as Wishy's had been and could be ended just as easily. "Our original plans have therefore changed. Tonight, we will all receive a good sleep and begin our journey before the sun is up. Until that time, please feel free to enjoy the comforts of my home and relax. But," he emphasized, "please be aware of my cardinal rule. I have come to grow fond of each and every one of you; and I would consider it a great personal tragedy to have to kill you." He paused. "You will find my staff very friendly and accommodating. Feel free to ask them for assistance. But if you try to escape, they will kill you…with a smile, of course."

With that, we all went our separate ways. Kringle and Big Nose found the game room and decided to shoot some pool. Juan went into the kitchen to ask the cook if he could get the recipe for her braised duck sauce, which was indeed superb. Linebacker went into his office to tend to whatever business killers and thieves need tend to. Iris excused herself to her room, and I wandered out into the garden under the watchful eyes of our "protectors." Looking around, I saw that the compound was really well designed for security. There were cameras everywhere and very few, if any, dark corners in which someone wanting to scale the high wall could wait until the opportunity appeared to make his move. Those trees that were somewhat near to the wall had all the branches on that side of the tree removed, and I could see no branches dangling over the wall from the outside. I dismissed whatever fantasies I'd had about leaving. I could see one or two night birds zooming in and out of the floodlights. Gulls, possibly? Always looking for my black belted friend, I chuckled to myself.

"They sometimes fly at night," came Iris's familiar soft voice from behind me.

"Yes. So I've noticed. Not too many gulls in Des Moines. One of them is a friend of mine."

"A friend?"

"Yes." I chuckled. "He's got a band of dirty feathers right around the middle of his body. I noticed him back on the yacht. Then again, over on the island."

As she drew closer, I could sense a hint of perfume—not too much, just a hint. It was captivating. We began strolling through the garden, stopping by a tree near a small fountain.

"Jimmy, are they going to kill us?" There was no terror in her eyes now. Not like on the yacht during the storm. It was like a woman who had come to grips with a terminal illness. She just needed to say what she had to say first.

As I am wont to do regularly, I uttered my first reaction, trying to allay her concerns. "Oh, no. No, Iris. They're not going to kill us. No." She looked at me like she knew I was lying to her, which I was. "Well," I said, changing my tone. "I don't know, sweetheart. I don't know. I hope not." I looked into her eyes, eyes so big and so deep; I could see men still wandering in them, trying to find their way out. "Especially now," I added. This time when our lips met and our bodies crushed together, there was no consternation, no doubts, no second thoughts about the world or the people around us. There was just us.

Breakfast at 3:00 AM was something I hadn't done in years, since that fishing trip to the wilds of Northern Wisconsin, near the Michigan border. Bunch of guys from college wanted a week in the woods…real woods. We caught a few, some tasty trout, some wall-eyes and a bunch of bony northern pikes. But mostly, the guys just caught bottle bass. It was a good time.

Iris sat next to me at the breakfast table. Big Nose didn't care and apparently neither did the others. At that point, it wouldn't have made any difference to us, if they had. I asked Linebacker about the cross. He told me it was secured in a safe. I told him I needed it to find the church and the treasure. He seemed skeptical but agreed.

Following breakfast, another good sign they might not kill us. We were blindfolded again and put into a convoy of three automobiles with tinted windows. I'm guessing some forty minutes or so later, we stopped at a small airport, where our blindfolds were removed, and we were loaded onto a twin-engine Beechcraft Model 99, fifteen-passenger aircraft. How did I know all that? I read the information packet on the back of the seat.

Linebacker addressed us. "Your attention, please, mes amis. We will be in flight for approximately one and one-half hours. You will no longer require blindfolds. But again, I must warn you that your every move will be monitored, and any violation of my cardinal rule will be dealt with immediately and with no further warning." He paused briefly. "Is that understood?" We all acknowledged. "Good," he smiled. "Enjoy your flight."

Some of us welcomed the extra hour and a half sleep. The rough landing on a dirt airstrip woke me up. As we stepped out of the plane, the jungle heat slammed into our senses like a tidal wave of hot steam; worse even than Cocos Island, where there was at least an occasional sea breeze. I looked around. Green. Except for the blue sky and the dirt landing strip, that was it. Three Land Rovers were waiting at the edge of the runway. Workers were already unloading gear from the plane and piling it into the Rovers. If these killers were to put half of their organizational skills into world peace, we'd never have a war. Juan, Iris, and I were directed to the first waiting Rover. As we walked toward it, there being nobody within earshot, we talked.

"Know where we are, Juan?" I asked.

"Si, senor. I have been here before...on school trips."

"Know of any churches around here?"

"No, senor. This is a tourist area. People come to see the clay licks...and Machu Picchu."

"Machu Picchu, huh? I've always wanted to see that myself. I wonder if they'll let us sightsee?" They both laughed at my facetious comment.

Iris chimed in. "Jimmy, what if we can attract the attention of some tourists? Maybe they could tell the authorities."

"Right," I answered. "And maybe we could end up as alligator treats too."

"Senor," Juan asked, "what did the book say about where we go from the clay licks?"

My answer startled both of them. "Nothing. It stopped at the clay licks. I don't have a clue which direction to go from there."

"But," stammered Iris, "I thought you told him you needed the cross to help find the church?"

"I did. I lied. I need the cross to bring back to the church, but it said nothing in the book about how to find it from the clay licks."

"Oh, wow," said Juan. "We are in deep kimchi now, senor."

Just then, I felt something small and wet and sticky land on my head, as a seagull swooped over, screeching loudly.

"Is that a gull?" Iris was incredulous. "What the hell is a gull doing…." She looked at Juan. "How far are we from the coast?"

"At least four hundred miles, senora."

"What the hell is he doing four hundred miles from the coast? Is he lost?"

I broke into a wide grin and a sigh of relief, as I saw the belt of dirty feathers around its body and wiped its beautiful poop off my head. My hope beyond hope was confirmed. "Nope. He's not lost. We are. He knows exactly where he's going, and we are going to follow him."

When Linebacker joined us in the Rover, I told him that I would need to stop periodically and get my bearings once we've reached the clay licks.

"Monsieur," he answered, "I don't care if you want to stop and do pirouettes in a tutu if it will lead us to a hundred-million-dollar treasure."

Since there were no roads to speak of in the area—this being a protected national park—the trip to the clay licks was arduous, to say the least. Now I understood, why the Land Rovers? It took us nearly half a day to go the forty-odd miles to the Macaw Clay Licks, Manu. We were on the east side of the Rio Madre de Dios, the Mother of God River, and the clay licks were in a flood plain area on the west side. Juan had visited there many times, and he assured us that we were in the correct location, which coordinated well with Linebacker's map. Desperately, I looked around for my friend, the dirty gull.

Linebacker was becoming impatient. "Well, Monsieur Hudson, where do we go from here?"

If this experience taught me nothing else, it taught me to lie on my feet. "Yes. Well. For this, I need the cross, please." He handed it to me, and I held it up toward the east, trying to think up a good story to quell Linebacker's anger until my friend showed up. "The sun. The sun is not right yet. The sun has to be behind us to cast the right shadow."

"Again, with the games, Monsieur Hudson! Do not play them with me!" He put his hand on his gun. Then a stroke of poetic justice happened…right on top of Linebacker's forehead. Yup. He got creamed by my good friend with the dirty feathers. "Sacré bleu!" I could not help but break out in uproarious laughter.

Before Linebacker could recover enough to shoot me, I pointed in the easterly direction my friend had flown. "That way," I said. Linebacker turned and ordered us all back into the Rovers. This was the first chance I'd had to actually count the number of bodies in our expedition. There were five hostages, and Linebacker had brought five armed guards, one of them being a female from the compound. She was apparently there to make Iris feel more comfortable about bathroom breaks and such. I wondered how a vicious killer could be so considerate.

As we drove east, what little trail there was became no trail at all, and soon, even the Rovers could go no farther. Linebacker got out.

"All right. From this point, we go on foot," I declared. He looked daggers at me. I smiled, maybe just to get his goat a little. Looking back down the trail, I saw none. Huh? Was it just my imagination, or had the trail closed up behind us? I shook my head to clear it. No. I just wasn't paying attention, as we drove. Looking up, I saw my friend still flying back and forth in an easterly direction. I turned to Juan.

"Juan, we're going roughly in an easterly direction. Do you know of anything out this way?"

"Machu Picchu," he answered. Whoa! Things were getting more and more weird all the time. Then, I remembered something out of the book that I'd forgotten. Grandfather had said, "Salvation lies between a rainbow and the city that isn't." It didn't make any sense then, but now it did. The rainbow being the clay licks and the city that isn't being Machu Picchu. That city was abandoned sometime after the conquistadors decimated the area, although there's no evidence to prove that's why the inhabitants left or even that the conquistadors had entered the city. Some believe it was a plague that forced the people out...or killed them off. Whatever the reason, one could say that a city is not a city without inhabitants. An abstract assumption to be sure.

As we got deeper, the jungle got thicker; and soon, the guards were taking turns hacking through the thick underbrush with machetes. The other areas we'd gone through didn't seem to be anywhere near this bad. Something else was happening also, something almost intangible. The sense of isolation grew around us, more than just the jungle. It seemed as if we were no longer in the here and now; we were somewhere else, some time else. The expedition began to get jumpy, irritable...frightened. After an hour of grueling going, Linebacker called for a break.

"We will rest here. Please remember to drink copious amounts of water. Dehydration is a sneaky killer," he said. That's as opposed to Linebacker himself who was an up-front, look-you-in-the-eye-and-blow-your-brains-out killer.

Not wanting to cause the ladies any embarrassment, I told Linebacker I was going a few yards out into the bushes to relieve myself. He looked over at Iris, thereby telling me she was toast if I decided not to come back. I gave him an understanding nod, and he nodded his permission. I set out, comfort equipment in hand. Now, it would be rude and crude of me to detail this excursion, so I won't. I only mention it because of what happened on my return trip. After washing my hands as thoroughly as possible under the circumstances, I started back, watching where I put my feet, to avoid ankle twists and snakebites. I began to get the feeling I was not alone. Looking up, out of the corner of my eye, I saw a native, an Indian...perhaps an Inca. He was about twenty yards away, wearing a thong, a colorful headdress, and carrying a blowgun with a small quiver full of darts. That was frightening enough, but what sat beside him made my blood run cold. Beside him was the largest black panther my baby green and blue had ever seen. He just sat there, watching me, they both were. Speechless, I stumbled my way back to our rest stop.

# The ancient ones...the deadly ones

Juan noticed how pale I'd become. "What is the matter, Senor Hudson? You look as if you had just seen a ghost."

"I hope it was," came my honest answer. "I hope it was. I'll tell you about it later." Linebacker approached me...and he wasn't smiling. His eyes were cold, and his jaw was set.

"Monsieur Hudson," he cautioned. "I have reached the limits of my endurance. I will give you thirty more minutes to lead us to this treasure. If you fail, I will kill one of you every thirty minutes until you do...beginning with her." He nodded toward Iris. "Do we understand each other, monsieur?" I nodded compliance. "Good. Now, let us resume."

Through each foot of jungle we labored, I wracked my brain to come up with some way to delay the ominous threat I knew he meant. Why was I drawing such a blank now, when I needed it the most? Linebacker stopped us and barked some orders in Spanish to his henchmen. They each held a gun to our individual heads. I looked over at a terrified Iris, whose matron was holding a cocked pistol to Iris's head.

"Monsieur Hudson," he shouted, "I warned you!"

"NO!" I screamed at the top of my lungs.

All eyes were on Iris. Kringle must have thought it an opportune time to make good his escape. No sooner had I screamed, then Kringle chopped the gun out of his guard's hand, picked it up, fired a bullet through the man's head and turned to run. He hadn't gotten four steps before a firing squad ripped into him. Linebacker was furious. He shrieked as he turned around, his gun leveling at Iris.

"KILL H…!" His words turned to blood, as a poison dart penetrated his throat, another his neck and still a third, his heart. In less time than it takes to tell, the steamy jungle air was thick with flying death, all of them aimed at our captors. The poison's paralyzing power was nearly instantaneous. Within seconds of feeling the sting of penetration, the victim's body stiffened, cries of anguish were cut short, and they fell nearly where they stood. As I lunged for Iris, I saw Big Nose dive between a large log and a rock, the darts bouncing off the rock or lodging in the log.

As quickly as it had started, it was finished. Our unseen saviors had melted back into…into what? Was it the primordial forest to which they returned, or could it have been…time? The answer is as vaporous as their ghostly breath that had filled the air with deadly darts. From where Iris and I had landed on the ground, I looked over at Juan. He was frozen stiff with fear…or poison. No. He didn't seem to have been the target of their onslaught, only our captors, our greedy killers, whose hearts were not true, were the ones chosen to die. They were the targets. Big Nose got lucky. Sticking his head up above the log, he spotted the cross, still in Linebacker's belt, and made a beeline to retrieve it.

"Juan!" I tried to warn Juan, but Big Nose had already grabbed the cross and raced past him, knocking him down in the process. "Stop him!" Still in a state of confusion, Big Nose's disoriented mind paid no attention to which direction he was running, and he disappeared into the jungle in an easterly direction, just the opposite of what he should have done. Seeing that Iris was all right, I took out after Big Nose with Juan and Iris close behind.

I may say that Big Nose was not the only emotional victim of everything that had transpired over the last few minutes. Like a maniac, I broke, pushed and threw any branch that dare interfere with my crusade to save that cross and Grandfather Hudson's immortal soul. Of course, in such a destructive mental state, my feet were as confused as my brain, and I soon found my face buried into the musty, rotting earth. I had heretofore made great conscious efforts to keep my wits about me, to concentrate on the task at hand, no matter what the situation. I must say now, those efforts ended that day on the floor of the Amazon jungle in Peru at approximately 3:00 PM.

Tears flooded the ground on which I lay, as my fist pounded its frustration into the earth. I suppose I was blaming God for my misfortune, as we all have a tendency to do now and then. I kept begging for Grandfather's forgiveness.

"Oh, God, Grandfather! I am so sorry! I am so sorry! I failed you, Grandfather. Please forgive me, Grandfather. I am so sorry." And that's how Iris and Juan found me; a babbling, blathering pile of passionate self-pity. After the initial shock of seeing me like this, they tried to calm me down, with little success, until...

The stifling, still jungle air fairly shook with a low guttural growl that fluttered the leaves with fear. Birds took to flight and prey of all kind scattered in terror. Fast on the heels of this hellish tone came the terrified scream of a man, a familiar man, one whom I had despised. But even Big Nose didn't deserve a death like that. Nobody did. Well, maybe Linebacker. The struggle must have been brief, since Big Nose hadn't even been able to produce another panicked scream before the animal ripped him apart.

The three of us looked toward the edge of a small clearing, some twenty yards or so away. We all knew who it was and what had happened. The question was, did we have the courage to go there? I remembered my encounter with the Inca warrior. Yes. That had to be it. The cat or the warrior could have killed me then but didn't. I got up, brushed myself off and started for the clearing. Iris and Juan were shocked.

"Jimmy! Jimmy, where are you going? You can't go out there. It'll kill you! Jimmy!"

"Senor Hudson, you cannot! I beg of you. Stay here."

I stopped and looked back at them with just a wry little grin. "Na. He won't hurt me. He's my bud. We're old friends. Known him for years." Then I continued into the clearing. What I saw I will not, out of respect for the dead, describe. Suffice it to say that Big Nose still clutched the cross in what was left of his hand. My eyes were riveted on the panther, which was still hovering over its kill. It looked at me. The warrior stood by its side and stared into my eyes. They were not the eyes of the dead. There was life in them and kindness and fierceness and all those things we feel when we are alive. I felt comfortable. There was no fear. He nodded slightly. Slowly, cautiously, I knelt down, grabbing the cross in one hand and Big Nose's wrist with the other. The blood that was everywhere made the gold cross slick, and it pulled through his death-clenched hand without a struggle. Taking out my handkerchief, I began wiping off the blood. I heard Iris and Juan coming up behind me.

"What the..." She could not finish the sentence.

"Ay ¡caramba!"

I turned to look at them. They were not looking at me. They were looking into the distance...the distant past, as it were. I turned back and looked up. I guess that, being so wrapped up in the warrior, the cat and the cross, I didn't notice the village full of huts and people...and one church. To say the scene was like something out of a movie is trite...but it was. A half dozen small, round thatched huts lined the perimeter of the clearing. In the center was a large square building. The walls were of some type of adobe with two glassless windows on each side and a thatched roof. Above the door was a wooden cross. And the people. The people, I was sure, had just stepped off the pages of a *National Geographic Magazine*; you know, the kind young boys like to look at because they have half-na-ked women in them. Except of course, these villagers were not going about their daily routines. They were instead all gathered about and staring silently directly at me and the cross.

"Jimmy," Iris asked, "where did these people come from? What the hell is going on here?"

I didn't answer. I looked over at the warrior who nodded again. Silently, as if in a funeral procession, I began walking toward the door of the church, cross out in front of me; maybe it was to show them I was fulfilling my promise to Grandfather Hudson. I entered the church slowly, solemnly, with Iris and Juan close behind. There were villagers sitting on rough log benches. Their innocent, hopeful stares followed us, as we walked up the aisle to the altar, which was also made of rough-hewn logs and covered with a white silk altar cloth, adorned with a red embroidered cross on the front. Two brass or gold candlesticks were on each side of a raised platform on which the cross should have been. At one end of the altar stood an elderly priest in simple vestments; at the opposite end stood my friend, the warrior, and his panther. I didn't stop to wonder how he had gotten there ahead of me; I just accepted it. After the things I'd experienced in the last couple of weeks, I stopped asking "why" all the time and just accepted that it was. A very peaceful feeling.

Nobody spoke. Nobody had to, save perhaps for Iris and Juan; and they were too dumbfounded to speak. The kind eyes of the priest met mine, and he nodded ever so slightly. There went that dog, poo-pin' tacks again. My hands began to shake uncontrollably, as I rev-erently inserted the base of the cross into its long-empty stand. The priest smiled, made the sign of the cross and folded his hands, as if in a prayer of thanks. I looked around, waiting for some further reaction from him, from the congregation, from the warrior...from *somebody*. No acclamations were made. Then, something did hap-pen. They began to disappear...all of them. Not all at once, though. They seemed to melt away; to dissolve, as Grandfather did after the first conversation we had. In a matter of seconds, they were gone... all gone.

I turned to look at Iris and Juan. They were awestruck. As my dear sainted grandmother would say, they didn't know whether to jump up or sit down. They didn't have time to do either. I wondered if I had now set Great-Great-Great-Grandfather Hudson's soul free at last. That question was answered anon when the back wall behind the altar began to open. Not "open," as in move; "open" as in simply disappear, to open a portal, a doorway into and out of the nether world. What did it look like? I truly do not know for sure. To me, it looked to be a great void, which began filling with an ever-changing rainbow of lights and mist from which scenes would appear and disappear aimlessly. There was no sound, only ghostly movement in an ocean of light and color. I say I do not know because Iris and Juan each saw something different. Perhaps our preconceived perception of whatever afterlife may or may not exist morphed it into what we wanted it to be.

The reality, if indeed it was real, of what it looked like did not matter, once I saw a now-familiar figure walking out of the mist to greet me, followed by a small entourage; a lovely, raven-haired woman, two children—male and female—and a blonde-haired young lady whose attire appeared to be that of a maid or a cook. Grandfather Hudson now looked free from strife, there among the peaceful dead. His smile emanated love and gratitude for his salvation from the nothingness of purgatory. He walked with purpose, with confidence, as he extended his hand toward mine. In my encounters with Grandfather, I had never actually touched him. Indeed, I had no way of knowing if he had only been a figment of my imagination; until the time when Hudson flesh gripped Hudson flesh. It was then I knew I had not been dreaming or delusional. It was then I knew Grandfather Hudson had been—and was—real. Tears began to well up again as Grandfather and I embraced, our love and respect for each other falling shamelessly on each other's shoulder. Tears really can cleanse the soul and replace a thousand thank-you's.

When the tears were gone, we separated, and he gave voice to those tears. "Thank you, James. Thank you so much, not only for myself, but for my family."

I smiled. "You called me... James."

"That is your name, isn't it?"

"Yes, it is, Grandfather. But you always called me boy before."

"You are no longer a boy in my eyes, James. You are a man."

"Yes. I think I understand that now, Grandfather."

"Being a man has less to do with your age than it does with what's in your heart, James. And your heart is pure and true, just like I knew it would be."

"Thank you, Grandfather."

He paused and turned to introduce me to his entourage. "These are the people in my family and my life." They said nothing and made no moves toward us. The lovely raven-haired woman and the children I recognized from photos in his house...er, my house...well, our house.

"I know who they are," I said. "Great-Great-Great-Grandmother Marion, Althea, and James Bartholomew Hudson the Second."

"Yes. That is correct."

"And let me guess," I said, shifting my gaze to the blonde servant. "This would be the cook who served you faithfully for many years?"

Grandfather caught the double entendre and smiled sheepishly. "Yes. This is Gertrude. She's as much a part of our family as anybody." Gertrude smiled politely and made a little curtsy. I looked at Marion to see if there were any reaction to the introduction of what must have been her rival for Grandfather's affections. There was none. But times were different then. Mistresses and lovers were not only common but expected in some circles. About that time, like Long John Silver's parrot, my friend the gull with the dirty feathers flew through the window and perched on Grandfather's shoulder. We both laughed. No explanation necessary.

I paused. "Grandfather?"

"Yes, James?"

"Can you tell me how it happened? I mean, how did you come to be stuck where you were so long?"

"Aye," he said reflectively. "I do owe ye that explanation, don't I?" He paused a while, took a deep breath, then plunged into his story. "I wasn't always a pirate, James. I was a peddler. I sold and bartered pots and pans and trinkets to the Indians and the mission-aries. I guess I wasn't much of a salesman because I was hungry a lot…and lonely. I'd heard of a mission that was deep in the jungle, near some old ruins that had been forgotten by time. It was said to contain riches untold. I hired some Indians to guide me in search of it. Halfway there, they were scared off by rumors of a fierce tribe that feasted on human flesh. I wandered for days in the jungle and finally collapsed from hunger, exhaustion and fever." He paused for reflection and then continued.

"When I awoke, I was in a native hut being tended by a priest…a Catholic priest, Father Alejandro. He nursed me back to health, fed me and gave me clean clothes to wear…just as our Savior said he should." His voice trailed off a bit as he became more pensive, then he continued afresh. "But I was just a lad, not much older than young Juan here. I was tired of being poor, tired of being lonely and tired of the constant struggles of life. I wanted more." Again, a pause to take a deep breath. "So, one evening, I snuck into the church and stole the cross, intending to sell it in Lima. But Father Alejandro and Chief Oscollo…"

I interrupted him. "The warrior with the panther."

"Yes," he said, then continued. "As I was saying, they came upon me just as I was about to leave the church. Chief Oscollo was about to order his cat to attack me, but Father Alejandro stopped him." At this point, something beyond Grandfather caught my eye. Behind him, behind his entourage, there seemed to be playing out everything Grandfather was telling me, almost like a three-dimensional screen at a cinema. There was not a sound, but the actions were unmistakable and even a little bit eerie. I watched what my grandfather did as a young man, even as he was telling me. Wow.

"Father Alejandro would not let them kill me. He told me that I was not stealing from him, I was stealing from God; and that, should I continue with this transgression, my soul would never find peace until I alone had returned the cross to its rightful place in God's universe."

I interrupted him again. "Which you could not do after you died. So, you needed a descendant named James Bartholomew Hudson to return the cross and fulfill the requirement."

"Yes."

"And when your only son died prematurely, you were stuck there in purgatory until another descendant was named after you and could return the cross for you."

"Yes. But I thought about none of that at the time. I was young, and I was stupid...as most men are wont to be at that age. All I wanted was to return to Lima and claim my fortune. That is what I meant, when I warned you about greed taking over your soul, James."

"Yes. I remember that; and I almost gave in to it...almost."

"Almost is...almost," he continued. "When I finally made it back to Lima, the city was in a panic. Bolivar's forces were expected to conquer all of South America, including Lima. All the nobles and all the churches were gathering their treasures to either hide or ship away to a safe place. I ended up shipping aboard a sloop, the *Mary Deare*, as a cook's helper. The captain's name was Thompson, a despicable human being. We were to transport as much of the gold and jewels from the churches of Lima as we could carry back to Spain. Of course, you know it never made it there. On the third day out, Captain ordered every member of the crew to participate in slaughtering the guards and the priests that were on board and throwing their bodies to the sharks. The priests, James; we murdered priests."

"And did you participate?"

"Aye. To my shame, but I did not kill anybody. Whenever I aimed my pistol, I made sure to aim where it would not kill. From that, I got the reputation of being a very bad shot. Something they could believe of a cook's helper. I knew someone else would kill them, and if I didn't participate at all, I myself would be killed."

"So, you never killed anybody as a pirate?"

"Oh yes. I had to. But it was only in self-defense, when somebody was about to kill me."

"Are you as bad a shot as you pretended to be?"

He chuckled. "Well, I could knock the tail end of a firefly at eighty feet...when he's on the wing."

I laughed. "You were there when they buried the treasure on Cocos Island, then?"

"Aye. That, I was. When they found me with the cross, they thought I had stolen it from the treasure on board, and they were going to kill me. I used every wily trick in the book to convince them otherwise. In the end, I asked captain if I could bury the cross where it could stand guard over the rest of the treasure. He agreed. The rock wall was too hard to dig out a hole in it, so I chiseled a cross on it and buried the gold cross at the bottom."

"So, what happened to the treasure, Grandfather?"

"I don't rightly know, James. I'm guessing one of the other crew came back and removed it, but didn't bother with or know about the cross."

"What about the gold and jewels you left for me in the bank?"

"My share of subsequent pirating efforts, James. I'd like to say I quit after we hid the Lima treasure, but I didn't. I kept at it until I got old enough to realize what I was doing and the sins I was committing. And when I did quit, I had to feign illness to justify it with the captain. Quitters are dangerous people to a pirate captain, James. Ye leaves 'em knowing secrets other people would pay good money to know."

"There is no more treasure, Grandfather?"

"Would it make a difference, James? Knowing that, would ye have still taken on this task for me? Or would ye have thought it not lucrative enough?"

"You know I would have, Grandfather."

"Yes. Yes, I do, James." He paused. "And now, our time here is finished. We will not meet again, for at least another fifty or sixty years...I hope." As he spoke, he and his entourage began receding back into the nether world. As they did so, the brightest white light I'd ever seen appeared behind them.

"Goodbye, Grandfather." I choked back my tears. "I love you."

"Goodbye, James Bartholomew Hudson the Third. I love you too." His words trailed off. "And remember, just as beautiful things can be ugly on the inside, so too can ugly be beautiful on the inside."

With that, the portal into that celestial spirit world from which all of us originate and to which we return closed up. But that was not the end; well actually, it was nearly the end of all of us. Just as all the people from that bygone era disappeared and returned to their roots, so too did the church and the village. Logs and grass began to fall from the ceiling, and the walls began to crumble inward. I screamed as loud as I could, as I ran for the doorway, dragging Iris behind me. "Run!" Juan was the last out...and just in time too. When we emerged from the doorway, we found that thick brush and trees had swallowed up the church completely, and we had to fight our way through it, sustaining scratches and bruises by the time we had reached what little clearing was left. Had we not been inside the church when it reverted to its present state, we never would have known it was there at all. But we did make it out to safety...well, sort of.

I would like to know, what is it about me? Sure, I'm ugly, but that's not illegal...yet. I have seen pictures of John Dillinger, Baby Face Nelson, Jesse James, Machine Gun Kelly, and a whole bunch of other nasty criminals...and I don't look like any one of them. So, why is it that *I* am the one who's always getting the barrel of a gun shoved in his face? Hmmm? Why? I really would like to know. In this case, it was a whole bunch of guns...M16A1s, to be exact. They were wielded by a dozen or more soldiers in jungle fatigues and aimed directly at all three of us. Our hands shot straight into the air so fast I'm sure they could feel the breeze. One of them shouted something in Spanish.

Juan translated. "Down on the ground, senor, senora! Keep your hands out to your sides!" We did so with no hesitation. I could hear the whop, whop, whop of a helicopter; no, two; no, three, as they hovered over the small clearing. Taking a chance, I probably should not. I saw two men, one in jungle fatigues and one in black, repelling down from two of the UH-1, Hueys. "Keep your head down, senor!" That was Juan's voice. Presently, I heard another.

"Mister Hudson! It's all right! You can get up now! Nobody's going to shoot you!" Well, well. My dear old friend, Lieutenant Trevor. What the hell is he doing here in the middle of the Amazon jungle? When the Hueys departed, we could talk normally again. Normally? After the last two weeks, I had no idea what anything normal was.

We got up. Trevor was dressed all in black and was sporting a forty-five caliber in his holster. "Sorry to startle you, Mister Hudson," he said, taking off his repelling equipment. "We really were concerned about you after you all had been captured by real pirates, so we decided we'd better close in and call an end to the operation before somebody got hurt."

It slowly began to dawn on me that Trevor knew about everything that had transpired in the last couple of weeks...and said nothing...or done nothing. My blood began to run a little warm. "What the hell do you mean, 'somebody got hurt'?" I was not a happy camper. "Somebody got *dead;* several somebodies! And we were almost among them!"

"But you weren't, Mister Hudson."

"Just who the hell are you, Trevor? You owe me some explanations...now."

"I am sorry to report, Mister Hudson, that Police Lieutenant Trevor is dead. Killed in the line of duty. Tragic affair, it was."

"Excuse me? Then who the hell are you?"

"My name is not important. It's whatever you want it to be, I guess. I work for a very unknown department in the government. It lies somewhere in between the FBI and the CIA, but belongs to neither. We work with various countries on various cases around the world. This one happened to be the stolen treasure of Lima. We've been working with the Peruvian government, the Costa Rican government and the Vatican for a long time in an effort to track it down; but as you can see, have not had a lot of success."

"What about all the dead bodies that have piled up? How do you explain them?"

"They were criminals, Mister Hudson; killers. Criminals get killed all the time, and usually, nobody takes any note of it." He turned to Iris. "I do apologize, madam. I did not mean to make light of your husband's death, but he was deeply involved in Mister Jasper's murder."

"I had nothing to do with that, Lieutenant...or whoever you are."

"Yes. We've been investigating that, as has the FBI, and I'm sure you'll be vindicated...at least on that charge. Now, the kidnapping and fraud charges are another matter."

"How did you know Jasper was dead?"

"Blood samples we took from the floorboards and the steps in the attic. The blood seeped down through the cracks and settled in different places than the paint. The body washed up on shore twenty miles south of town."

I looked around at the soldiers who were now forming ranks to depart. "What about the Indians? Did you dress these guys up as Incas and give them blowguns?"

He looked puzzled. "Indians? What Incas? We haven't seen any indigenous tribes...and we certainly didn't dress anybody up like one."

I decided I'd better change the subject. "How did you track us so closely?"

"Well, we were doing pretty well up until the time the yacht left you on the island and was seized by pirates. We would check up on you periodically to make sure you weren't in any real danger."

My brain hit the light switch. "Ah! The Coast Guard inspection."

"Yes, of course. And the Park Rangers on the island. All just keeping an eye on you."

"So, what happens now?"

"Now, we put you all on a chopper and head back to Lima. I have straightened everything out with the Peruvian government. You will not be charged. Iris will be extradited to the United States to stand trial on kidnapping and fraud charges, and Juan will be returned to the orphanage."

Juan's heart sank, as did Iris's and mine. "Oh no, senor," he exclaimed, "you cannot do this! I will *not* return to that terrible place. I will not."

"It's not up to me, son," replied Trevor. "That's for the Peruvian government to decide. Besides, there's the little matter of the director's broken nose to deal with."

I scowled just slightly at Juan, more like a parent feigning irritation for something he probably would have done himself. A parent? A parent? No. Get thee behind me!

"You didn't tell me about that," I said.

"I was afraid to, senor. I was afraid you would be angry."

"Well," I said in my sternest daddy voice, "we'll discuss that later."

# CHAPTER TWELVE

Later came in yet another world. Lima. A few weeks earlier, I had been a struggling substitute teacher from Corn Belt, USA. I had no intention of becoming a homeowner a detective a treasure hunter a kidnap victim a fighter, a swashbuckling sailor, an explorer, and a dabbler in the occult. Now, I'm about to become a daddy and, God help me, maybe a husband. What the hell happened to me? I would imagine that is something a huge majority of men ask themselves at one point or another in their lives. There is no answer other than life happened to me, just as it has happened since the beginning of humankind, when we crawled out of the sea and began to walk upright. Just as it happened for those ancient villagers we did not see. Juan, Iris, and I decided that our encounters with the Indians and in the church would remain forever ours. Nobody would believe us anyway.

The modern world of Lima took a little getting used to. There were no snakes; except attorneys, no panthers; except in a zoo, no pirates; except for politicians and no jungles; except the concrete ones. "Hmmm," I thought, as I looked out over the city from my hotel room. "One jungle to another. Only the predators are different."

With the help of the U.S. Embassy, I procured an attorney to begin adoption proceedings for Juan Carlos Manuel Fernando Moralez…Hudson. The attorney was reputed to be one of the best in the country. I hoped so for what he was costing. But he said he could grease some wheels—for a price—to cut the normal adoption time down from two years to less than a year. Until such time as that is finalized, Juan would be staying in a foster home and attending school. In the summer and during breaks, he would be staying with me. The assault charges against him were dropped, and the orphanage director subsequently was indicted on child abuse and theft charges and is awaiting trial. My expensive attorney assured me that Juan's foster home would be of the finest quality...his, for a price.

The tough part of Lima was saying goodbye to Iris. Seeing her cuffed to a matron, ready to board a plane to the States, was tearing me to pieces. But I knew things could have been worse. At least she wasn't an accessory to murder. I called a friend of mine back in Des Moines. He's partners in a law firm there. Knows everybody. He said he would try to get one of the best trial lawyers in the country to take her case. Two weeks later, I was boarding a plane for America myself. First, I went back to Des Moines to finalize Iris's defense team, then flew...home. Hmmm. Home. Sounds strange. I never had a home of my own before. Of course, I've never had a pending son and wife either.

As I entered my new/old home, I took stock of what I had done and what it had done to me. I certainly was not the same James Bartholomew Hudson the Third I had been. Things change us... sometimes for the better and sometimes not. I still haven't sorted out which way I have gone. Having a gun shoved in my face or seeing the ocean rising up to fill my lungs or feeling helpless and unable to move as an animal is about to clamp its jaws into my throat brought fear on a level that I had never known before, and frankly never want to know again. Watching the blood spurt from somebody's head or throat, as it is penetrated by a bullet or a poison dart turned my stomach in a way I can never forget. Life is so precious.

Conversely, the comfort of a friendship that can never be broken with someone who has shared all these experiences—including saving my life—and with whom I share a trust unshakable is priceless. That is why I decided to ask Juan if he would like to share my home and become part of my family. He said he had never, in his most joyful dreams, ever expected to have a family again; and then he cried (something he will kill me for saying, but that's how much he wanted it).

Finally, the reawakening of a part of my heart that I thought had died years ago to blossom full and rich and sweet; this is a sensation most men only know once...and many not at all. To have somebody so ever present with me, even when she isn't, can only be an indication of that motherload of feelings for which we all search, but so very few actually find. And then, the question always remains, is it gold or is it fool's gold? More often than not, the latter; but to quit searching is to quit living.

These things and more I pondered, sitting in my new/old house on my new/old love seat with my back nestled comfortably in Wafer Bay. Still, there were worrisome things I had to think about. Such a fine old house requires a great deal of maintenance and loving care... just as we do. The something less than a million dollars Grandfather left me had been dwindling fast. Taxes on it and the house were due. The lack of modern amenities would soon force me into mortgage to update with air conditioning and proper heat. Greasing all the wheels I needed to in Lima for Juan's adoption was costing me a bundle, and one of the finest trial lawyers in America does not work pro bono. Juan would need schooling—colleges are not cheap; and Iris...well, I wanted Iris to not have to worry about all those things over which wives and mothers fret, when their family's income falls so far short of necessary expenditures.

With these weighing heavily on my mind, my mood began to change. I started mulling over in my muddled mind ways I might tackle these pending pitfalls, and the more I mulled, the more muddled I became. Perhaps it had been a mistake to offer Juan something I wasn't sure I could give him. What if Iris isn't happy with me? Divorces are expensive also. Maybe we would need to keep operating the fleabag motel she inherited that barely makes a profit? What if... what if...what if. Those two words are probably responsible for the death of more dreams throughout time than any others. Still, they haunt us day and night.

I decided to wander up to the attic to see if there were any antique treasures that might be worth a few bucks, all the while knowing anything I might come across would only be a temporary fix for a long-term problem. Yes, there were those items that had tickled my fancy on my first visits up to this den of antiquity, but their values could not come close to what I'd need. I checked out the casks that were up there and found only clothing on which the moths had made many a tasty meal. Dress forms. Pots. Pans. The more I dug, the more frustrated and worried I became. I know now that I was experiencing the kind of ulcer-producing, alcohol-consuming anguish over one's lot in life that is felt by millions of people throughout the world. I didn't stop to think of all I had accomplished and all that we, as a family, could accomplish together. I was scared, and it freaked me out.

Quite simply…I snapped. Everything in that attic and indeed the house represented on one hand, the ecstasy of being offered on a silver platter what most men would kill for—and some do; and the anguish of foreseeing it dwindle away on the other. In an uncharacteristic rage, I began throwing whatever was handy wherever I could do the most damage. Luckily, I missed that beautiful ship's wheel. But most other things suffered my disgraceful exhibition of ungrateful, self-centered wrath. Picking up that beautiful antique baseball bat, I began pummeling…whom? Again, I was the victim of my own selfish anger with God for my being in this situation. We humans can be *so* stupid.

My eye caught the gargoyle I had encountered on my first night there. I began screaming at him…her…it. "It's your fault, you big piece of…!" With that, I swung an uppercut to one of its wings; and when it connected, the shockwave that reverberated through my arms sent torrents of pain through my entire body, a punishment I now know I deserved. Chunks of masonry flew everywhere, some bouncing off the roof and falling back down…among the pieces of eight and silver coins and jewels and other things one might find in a pirate's treasure chest.

I smiled, then grinned, then laughed heartily. "Grandfather, you sly old pirate, you!" My mind flashed back to something he'd said in the church: "…so too can ugly be beautiful on the inside." Greedily, I began gathering up my riches and filling my pockets. Why? I don't know. It just seemed like the thing to do at the time, even though I owned the house and didn't need to sneak the treasure out. Picking up the official Boy Scouts of America flashlight I always took with me into the attic, I peered down the hollow body of my most maligned friend. It was indeed stuffed full of pirate treasure.

After I had calmed down a bit, I felt so ashamed of myself for being so self-indulgent in my self-inflicted misery. I vowed then to have my friend, the gargoyle that had saved my life and guarded my treasure, expertly restored to his original ugly/beautiful self. I also vowed to, within my budget and to the limits of my financial ability, do what I could to help those who have not been as lucky as I. Maybe to give back to the human race in Grandfather's name, some of what he had plundered in his impetuous youth.

Now. Here. Today, as I sit on this dock chronicling the accounts of my adventure and watching the sailing boats glide smoothly through the rays of a beautiful sunset, I can get a sense of what Grandfather and the others might have felt in taking to a life on the high seas. The salt has tainted my blood and I, who could never cross a Midwestern lake without becoming ill, now long for the feel of an undulating deck under my feet and the sound of a sail, as it flutters in the wind. I long to find whatever is on the other side of the world in which I live. The lure of pirate treasure is still strong. The Lima treasure is still unfound; and there are countless others that lie in some cave on some island or in the depths of the sea guarded by the ghosts of those who perished with it.

Iris was given eight months to serve and two years of probation on the fraud charge. The kidnapping charge was dropped, when I refused to press it. She is scheduled to be released soon. I don't know if Iris and I will last. I hope so; she's a remarkable lady. But I will say that, owing to my lack of self-discipline, I recently visited that cellblock in my psyche wherein I had imprisoned the painful memories of my unrequited love. Stopping outside the door, I steeled myself before peeking through the narrow window of her cell door to drink of her toxic beauty. It was empty.

In a stroke of luck, the sailing yacht, *Iris*, was recovered in Thailand and will be returned to its new owner...Iris. The adoption is scheduled to be finalized about the same time Iris is released. With luck, things could be back to normal, or abnormal, in the next couple of years. That would give the three of us time to more fully adjust to each other. Then I was thinking it might be a good idea for the three of us to take a little vacation cruise. I was reading an article about some new evidence that was found about the Lima treasure. Yes. A nice, relaxing sea cruise might be just the thing.

### T H E   E N D

# ABOUT THE AUTHOR

A native of Northern Wisconsin, Dale is a 1977 graduate of the University of Wisconsin-Superior with a major in speech communication and a minor in radio/television/film. He attended the University of Southern California Graduate School program toward an MFA in screenwriting.

He has always been fascinated by treasures, pirates and the sea. "A sometimes-lethal combination," he says.. The treasure of Lima, Peru "which is real" first captured his attention as a junior in high school and cemented itself in his mind. He thought how neat it would be to board a sloop and sail into a treasure-hunting adventure. Two of his favorite authors growing up were Sir Arthur Conan Doyle and Edgar Rice Burroughs. He loved their styles and their stories. The consummation of this fascination is A NICE, RELAXING SEA CRUISE.

As a screenwriter, his screenplay, ALAMO-DULUTH: Anatomy of a Lynching based on The Lynchings in Duluth by Michael Fedo was awarded the grand prize at the 2010 Screenwriting Expo in Los Angeles. In 2015, retitled as Hate Storm, it won the Screenplay of Merit award at the Catalina Film Festival. Jim Cirile of coverageink.com called it potential Oscar bait.

He has already begun the process of adapting A NICE, RELAXING SEA CRUISE to the big screen.

His website is, www.curlyvic.com .